HOLLY WEBB

EMILY FEATHER

and the Chest of Charms

SCHOLASTIC

First published in the UK in 2014 by Scholastic Children's Books
An imprint of Scholastic Ltd
Euston House, 24 Eversholt Street
London, NW1 1DB, UK
Registered office: Westfield Road, Southam, Warwickshire, CV47 0RA
SCHOLASTIC and associated logos are trademarks and/
or registered trademarks of Scholastic Inc.

Text copyright © Holly Webb, 2014

The right of Holly Webb to be identified as the author
of this work has been asserted by her.

Cover illustration © Rosie Wheeldon, 2014

ISBN 978 1 407 130941

A CIP catalogue record for this book
is available from the British Library.

Printed and bound by CPI Group (UK) Ltd, Croydon, CR0 4YY
Papers used by Scholastic Children's Books are made
from wood grown in sustainable forests.

1 3 5 7 9 10 8 6 4 2

www.scholastic.co.uk/zone

For Katie

1

"I love the holidays," Emily murmured, kicking off her flip-flops and stretching out her toes to the sunshine.

"I suppose." Her younger brother Robin sighed, and poked gently at an ant with the end of a grass stem. The ant froze, bewildered, and then scuttled away.

Emily stuck another grass stem into her book

to mark her page, and rolled over to look at him properly. "What, don't you?"

Robin shrugged. "Holidays are just a bit boring. Nothing to do. . ."

"I know! That's what's so nice about it. Not having to get up for school, no rushing around. . ."

"You *never* rush around," Robin snorted. "And if Lark and Lory didn't chase you out of the house, you'd be late for school every day."

Emily propped her chin on her hands. "Maybe," she admitted. Her big sisters were very good at organizing her, it was true. Emily just wasn't a morning person. She did like school, but it was so nice to have a change in the holidays – going to bed later, and not being woken up by Mum shouting up the stairs to her little attic room. This morning

she'd slept until the sunlight filtered through the wavy glass in her bedroom windows, and the soft, golden glow had woken her. It was blissful. And she had six whole weeks of it ahead, too.

"If you're bored now, and it's only the first week of the holidays, what are you going to be like by the end of August?" she asked Robin.

"I should think I'll probably have eaten my own toes by then," Robin muttered gloomily.

"You could always go – well, you know – back home. . ." Emily suggested. "To the fairy world. That wouldn't be boring."

Robin glared at her. "For a start, *no*. Mum and Dad would kill me. Haven't you learned enough to know that by now? And anyway, it isn't my home. I've never lived there. None of us have."

3

Emily nodded slowly. "I suppose not. I hadn't really thought of that." She picked another grass stem, and chewed it. "So, where do you actually belong? Here or there?"

"I don't know," Robin admitted. "I've always lived here. I only visit the other place."

"But doesn't it feel different when you're there? Doesn't it feel like that's where you're meant to be?" Emily asked him, curiously. "I mean, there you can be in your real form."

She glanced enviously at his shoulders, remembering the soft brownish-grey wings that folded round them so naturally. The wings were the main thing she envied Lark and Lory and Robin. Not just that they could fly, which was amazing enough, but the beauty of the wings

4

themselves – the soft colours of the feathers, the arching shapes they made and the way they spilled out of Lark and Lory and Robin's shoulders like a waterfall. And they were so soft, so strokable.

A few weeks earlier, Emily had found out that she had been adopted – that her father had found her abandoned down by the river and brought her home. It had been strange enough, to find out suddenly that her family weren't related to her at all, and that no one knew who her real parents were or where she'd come from. But that had only been the beginning. In her family, Emily wasn't the unusual one.

Her parents, little brother and older twin sisters were all fairies. In disguise. Her lovely

old house, the house she'd always known, was actually a gateway to a fairy world, full of strange and secret doors. The mirror on the landing at the top of the stairs had been occasionally used as a spyhole by a curious water sprite, and her family's pet dog wasn't just a dog either.

It had been a lot to get used to.

Emily wasn't sure that she would ever be used to it, actually. But she was mostly past the panicked, disbelieving stage. Now she was fascinated.

"I wish we could go back," she sighed to Robin. "To visit properly, though, not just because something's gone wrong. I want to see it all – that amazing river, and the forests – and not while I'm being chased through them. I want to look at things. To see all the people."

"But you've probably seen more of that world than I have," Robin pointed out. "Whenever I go, it's with Mum and Dad, and we're all dressed up, and it's like a big occasion – an official visit. I don't get to meet people, and talk to them like you have."

"The only people I got to talk to were trying to kidnap me," Emily protested. "And the next time I was being hunted by great enormous slavering dogs. I wish we could just sneak through one of the doors, but I'd be scared."

Once Emily had got over some of her amazement, she had bribed her dad with tea and chocolate muffins, and tried to get him to tell her exactly what was going on in their house and behind the doors. She still didn't know everything,

of course. She couldn't expect to find out about a whole world in the space of one cup of tea. But at least now she had some idea.

Her father had explained that he was a watchman. He was there to guard the doors, and to protect the two worlds from each other. Occasionally, before the doors had been sealed and guarded, those from the fairy world would try to tempt humans through them. There was something about humans – particularly human children – that kept the fairy elders young. It was some sort of energy, which Emily didn't really understand. But she knew it was true.

She had strayed through one of the doors, completely by accident, in a surge of anger and unhappiness after she had found out the truth

8

about her family. She had run up the stairs to hide away in her room, but her purple-painted bedroom door had opened to somewhere else – a beautiful, dangerous place, full of fairies who wanted to keep her. One of them, Lady Anstis, had tempted her to stay, offering her what looked like a bowl of the most delicious fruit. But it had been loaded with spells, and if Emily had eaten it, the fairy magic would have made human food seem tasteless and strange. Even if Emily had returned home, she would have wasted away.

The fairy Ladies, like Anstis, were growing more and more powerful, her father had explained. There was no queen of the fairies any longer – she had died years before – and the king ruled alone. So there was a constant battle between the

Ladies of his court. The ultimate prize would be to persuade him to marry again.

"If we went back—" Emily started to say.

"Which we won't," Robin snapped.

"I know! But if we did, do you think I could have a disguise, maybe? So that people there wouldn't recognize me?"

"I don't know. . ." Robin said thoughtfully. "Maybe, maybe not. They'd be able to sense that you were human whatever we made you look like, I think. And you're not just human, either. Not with your magic." He frowned. "I don't think they'd be able to mistake you for anyone else, Ems."

Emily ducked her head to hide her shy, delighted smile. She couldn't help it. It was when Robin had said "your magic". She knew that she didn't have

anything like the power that Lark and Lory and Robin did. But because her family hid their true origins, and lived as humans, her brothers and sisters couldn't actually *do* much magic anyway. They might slip in just a little smidge of it, here and there – Emily was sure that Lark and Lory used it on their hair, which was always perfect – but their parents could tell if they used any more than that – which meant trouble.

Still, even for Emily to have that tiny dusting of magic was more than she'd ever dreamed. She gave a little gulp of excitement as she thought about it. She hadn't been born with magic, like her brother and sisters, but it was just possible that she had borrowed some. . . She and Robin had decided that it must have come from growing

up in a house where magic was bulging out all over the place.

Sometimes Emily wondered how she had got as far as ten years old without realizing that she lived in a fairy stronghold. But then, she'd just taken all the odd little things as normal. The moving pictures in her windows were just daydreams, she'd thought. And the way her sisters' bedroom doors seemed to change colour with their mood was just the odd way the light fell on the landing. It wasn't magic.

Except it was, and now a little bit of it was inside her. Emily had made it stronger, too, by her two visits to the fairy land through the doors. The first time she'd gone had been an accident – just blundering through the wrong

door. But the second time, she had meant to do it.

A water sprite had helped Emily and Lark and Lory escape from Lady Anstis. She had shown them a doorway back to the human world. But she had paid dearly for her help. She was chased away from her river, and hunted through the lands. Emily had used her growing magic to force her way back to the fairy world and rescue Sasha, the water-sprite, from the huntsmen's hounds.

Emily had been returning Sacha's kindness by helping her escape. If she hadn't managed to drag Sasha away, the water sprite would eventually have tired and given in and died. Emily's tiny scrap of magic had saved her.

It had been scary but exciting. Emily still couldn't quite believe she'd actually done it.

"Are you *really* bored?" Emily asked Robin now, trying to sound casual.

He only growled in response, poking irritably at another innocent ant.

"Because I can think of one thing we could do."

"I've told you, we're not going through any doors! Even if the huntsmen didn't recognize you or your magic, it's still crazy dangerous, and we'd get in massive trouble."

"I don't mean that. I just wondered. . . If I've got magic in me now, do you think I could ever do anything with it?" She looked at him hopefully. "Could you teach me?"

Robin stared at her in surprise.

"I mean – didn't you ever have lessons in how to use your magic?" Emily asked him. "What spells to use? Special words? Anything like that?"

Robin shook his head. "No. It's just there. It's part of me, and if I want to use it I do. Except most of the time I don't, of course, because of Mum and Dad's stupid rules. I never had lessons. It doesn't really work like that."

Emily sighed. "Of course it doesn't. Oh, you're so *lucky!*"

"There are things you could learn," a quiet voice added, and Emily rolled over suddenly, peering up into the sunlight. There were sunspots in her eyes, and she was squinting against the glare, but it wasn't the light that made the girl in front of her glitter.

Sasha wasn't like Robin and the others, pretending to be human. She was in her full fairy form, and she shone. The long tunic she wore fell to her ankles, and swirled around her like pouring water, liquid and glinting. Her hair swirled too, blowing around her shoulders like waterweed in a fast-flowing stream, and her eyes were the silver-green of a sunlit river. No one could mistake her for anything but a water fairy.

Which was why she spent most of her time hidden in the garden pond.

Emily and Robin were hiding her, for the moment, until they could work out a good way to tell their parents what Emily had done. Emily was certain that she had been right to save Sasha, but her parents might not see it the same way.

16

Although her father worked as a writer on this side of the doors, his true job was to keep fairy people from crossing over to the human world. It would be his duty to send Sasha back, whatever the consequences.

Emily stared up at her, wide-eyed. "What things?" she asked. "Oh, and I brought you this," she added, picking up a little parcel wrapped in greaseproof paper, and holding it out to Sasha.

"Is it chocolate?" the water fairy asked eagerly, sitting down next to her, and unwrapping her gift. Her hair waved and coiled with excitement as she pulled out a fat, squidgy chocolate brownie.

"Did you bring one for me?" Robin demanded.

"No! You practically ate your weight in them yesterday. That's the only one left."

Sasha delicately broke off a small piece of the brownie, and nibbled at it. "Even if I could go back home, I don't think I would," she sighed. "Marsh marigold roots and watercress simply don't compare." She looked thoughtfully at Emily. "You know, I do wonder if you already put your magic into your cooking."

"Do you think so?" Emily smiled shyly. She was used to people telling her how good her cooking was, but this was different. "I don't do it on purpose."

"No, but magic is instinctive. As Robin said, we don't have to do 'spells' for it to happen. We just use it when we need it. And for you, I think the magic comes out when you cook. Especially for your family."

Emily nodded. "I suppose that makes sense. It is my favourite thing to do. That and draw."

Sasha broke off another piece of brownie, and chuckled as Robin watched her enviously. She put it in her mouth, and eyed him as she chewed. "Gorgeous. . . So what do you think about when you're cooking?"

Emily blinked at her. "Um. The recipe, I suppose."

"That can't be everything," Robin disagreed. "For a start most of the time you know the recipe off by heart anyway. I don't know why you can't ever get your times tables right."

"Different sort of remembering. I don't like maths." Emily shrugged. "Except when it's useful. I don't think tables are useful at all. But recipe maths is."

"So if you know the recipe, what else do you think about?" Sasha rolled her eyes, and handed a small chunk of brownie to Robin. "Now stop looking at me as though you're half-starved."

Emily stared out across the garden, past the pond where Sasha was living, to the thicket of trees that hid the fence and made their garden look as though it went on for ever. "I suppose I think about what the different ingredients taste like. And what they'll be like mixed together. And who's going to eat it. If there's anything I'm trying that's new, I'll be hoping it works."

"Mmmm." Sasha nodded. "Wishing, then."

"Is that what I do?" Emily asked doubtfully.

"Wishing is some of the most powerful magic there is," Sasha told her, smiling. She crumbled

the last little piece of the chocolate brownie in her hand, ignoring Robin's moan of protest, and held the crumbs out to Emily, tipping a little shower of them into her hand.

Emily gazed back at her worriedly. "What do I do with them?" she asked.

Sasha smiled. "Whatever you like. . . You made them for us, didn't you? So they're already mixed with your magic. Now turn them into something else. Anything you like."

Emily frowned down at the handful of crumbs, wondering how on earth she was supposed to do this. For Sasha and Robin it would be easy – they had so much power, and they knew what to do with it. She didn't feel like she had any.

"And be careful, Emily," Sasha added gently. "Don't use too much magic. You know your parents have forbidden Lark and Lory and Robin to use theirs. There are watchers on the other side of the doors, too. Don't show them what you can do."

Robin snorted. "I shouldn't think it's much of a risk. I mean, it's only Emily. She's hardly going to make enough magic for anyone to notice."

He wasn't being deliberately cruel, but his words stung, and Emily stared down at the crumbs in her hand furiously. She would show him! She was sick of being the feeble human sister who couldn't do anything except make cakes.

But what should she do? It was just a handful

of chocolatey crumbs. How was she supposed to turn them into something else? And what should the something else be? Her mind had gone blank.

Robin was yawning. He wasn't even bothering to *watch*.

Emily glared at her hand and decided to turn the crumbs back into a huge and particularly delicious cake, which she wouldn't give Robin any of. Unless he begged.

She gritted her teeth, and her nose scrunched up, and she tried desperately to focus every last bit of energy and power and herself that she could. She could *feel* it working. But so slowly, and so little. She needed more crumbs – there was only enough there to make a feast for a mouse. Emily

smiled to herself, as the little mouse wandered into her head, sniffing hopefully for chocolatey crumbs – a little chocolate-brown mouse, with a dusty cocoa-coloured coat. His fur was like the cocoa powder that covered Mum's favourite expensive truffles, the ones she said were only for grown-ups.

Something tickled her fingers, and Emily twitched in surprise. She stretched her fingers out star-like in front of her, and a mouse froze on her palm, his whiskers waving. Then he seemed to decide that Emily was safe, and he went on eating the few crumbs that were left in her hand. The rest of them had turned into his dark-chocolate fur, and beady little chocolate-chip eyes.

Emily sighed. It wasn't an enormous cake. It wasn't an enormous anything. In fact he was a particularly tiny mouse. She had got distracted in the midst of her magic-working, and this was what had happened.

"I didn't mean for it to be a mouse," she told Sasha sadly. "I was trying to make a cake."

But Robin was staring at the mouse, fascinated and envious. "You made him! I didn't know you could do that! He's perfect. . ." He reached out one thin forefinger and gently stroked the top of the mouse's head.

"But I didn't mean to!" Emily tried to explain again.

Sasha put an arm around her shoulders, wrapping Emily in water-coolness. "Emily, I

wasn't really expecting you to make anything at all. I thought the crumbs might change colour perhaps. I had no idea you could do so much."

"It was mostly because I was annoyed that Robin thought I couldn't," Emily admitted.

"Sorry," Robin murmured. "But even Lark or Lory would find it hard to conjure up a living creature, you know . . . out of almost nothing, Emily," he looked at her hopefully. "Do you like mice much?"

"Not that much." Emily looked down at the tiny mouse. "I mean, he's sweet. . . But I don't really want him in my room. Do you think he could live in the garden?"

"Can I have him? Please?" Robin begged. "I

really, really want him, and I'll look after him. He likes cake. I'll share with him."

Emily giggled, gently tipping her fingers so that the chocolate brownie crumbs and the chocolate brownie mouse, slid into Robin's hand.

"Maybe you need to make a cake," Robin told her seriously. "He still looks hungry to me." He slipped the tiny mouse into the pocket on the front of his T-shirt. "We're both hungry." He looked at his sister hopefully, and Emily got up, glancing at Sasha.

"So, it's just about wishing?" Emily asked.

Sasha nodded, as she wandered back through the long grass to the pond. "Wishing, and practice. I think you should practise on Robin. . ."

2

"That boy's here again!" Robin hissed to Emily, as he leaned over to look at what she was mixing up.

Emily swirled raspberries through the lemony cake mixture and admired the sharp pink streaks they made, then she glanced round at Robin. "What, that one Lory keeps complaining about?"

Robin sniffed. "She complains about him,

but she isn't making him go away. She likes him following her about. He's like a puppy."

"Don't let Lory hear you say that." Lark had wandered in, hauling Gruff along behind her by his collar. The huge dog's claws were practically digging grooves in the floorboards, and he was growling – one long, low growl that went on and on. "You can't stand that slimy boy either, can you?" Lark murmured to him, rubbing his ears sympathetically. "I wish I could growl too. But we'd get in trouble if I let you bite him."

Gruff slumped crossly under the kitchen table and went on growling – just a grumpy, thundery rumble that echoed up around their feet every so often. Lark sat down next to Emily, stuck a finger into the cake mixture, and licked it.

Emily batted at her with the wooden spoon. "Stop it. It's not done."

"I like it not cooked. Can I scrape out the bowl afterwards?" Lark flopped into a chair at the table, licking her fingers.

"Where's Lory?" Robin muttered.

"Still at the front door talking to Dan. I got bored." Lark shrugged.

Emily eyed her sideways. She wondered if Lark was jealous that Dan was following Lory round like a love-struck spaniel, and not her. It was the first time that either Lark or Lory had had a boyfriend – they'd just never bothered before. Lory had always said that the boys at school were all too stupid even to talk to, let alone spend any time with. Lark had just snorted

when Emily asked her if she liked any of the boys in her year.

It wasn't as if Lory had actually said this Dan was her boyfriend. But he kept coming round and leaning elegantly against the door frame, talking to her and fluttering his long eyelashes. Emily really envied him those eyelashes. He had dark blond hair and really green eyes, and a fan of dark eyelashes – which were really unnatural-looking, come to think of it – so much darker than his hair.

Emily swept her cake mixture into the tin, leaving some in the bowl, and handed Robin and Lark each a spoon. She took one as well and put the bowl on the table between the three of them.

"Do you think his eyelashes are real?" she asked, chasing a smidge of raspberry round the

31

side of the bowl. "They're even longer than yours and Lory's. And not blond like his hair."

Lark blinked. "Oooh. I don't know. Maybe. . ." She smiled, her eyes glinting wickedly. "Probably he wears mascara. Or he dyes them. Well done, Emily . . . I'll have to ask Lory."

So she did mind, then. Just a little. Enough to want to tease her twin about the boy who was keeping them apart.

The smell of lemony-raspberry cake began to fill the kitchen as they sat round the table companionably, clearing the bowl. The kitchen door was open and they could hear a soft whisper of voices from down the hallway, where Lory and the boy were still leaning together in the doorway.

Dan had started hanging around at the end of

the summer term. At first it had been funny – a joke between Lark and Lory – that this gormless boy always seemed to pop up whenever they were sitting chatting at school, or even if they went shopping in town at the weekends.

Emily and Robin had first seen him when they all met up on the way home from school one afternoon. Lark and Lory's school finished a bit later than their primary school did, but it was closer to the house, so Lark and Lory quite often caught up with Emily and Robin, and Emily's best friend Rachel.

That day, Lark had been giggling, but Lory was pink-cheeked and cross-looking. Even the tips of her ears had gone red where they showed through her feathery blonde hair.

"What's the matter?" Emily had asked, wondering if Lory had been told off at school. She looked as though she wanted to kick somebody, and she was always complaining about how unfair their teachers were. Some of them still called Lark and Lory by the wrong names, even after two years at the school. It drove them mad.

"Did Mrs Harris think that you were Lark, like she did last week?" Emily suggested, ready to sympathize, and trying to think of some good insults for the biology teacher.

"No. Stupid Dan Hargreaves. Again!"

"Who's he?" Robin asked. He'd been running ahead, like he always did – he got bored with Emily and Rachel gossiping about school. But he'd trotted back to run in circles round Lark

34

and Lory. Now that Emily knew they were fairies, she'd realized that Robin missed the company of his own people during the day at school. He always wanted to be close to his big sisters when they first met up again.

"No one you know," Lory growled crossly.

"A boy in our year," Lark explained. "He fancies Lory."

"Oh. Poor him." Robin smirked.

"And what's that supposed to mean?" Lory snapped.

"Nothing!" Robin danced backwards away from her. "Just that he'll be getting shouted at like that all the time, that's all!"

Lory muttered something furious and stomped on ahead, scowling.

"She sounds really upset," Emily said, watching Lory stalking up the road and kicking at the brownish grass on the edge of the pavement.

"Mmmm. He's been hanging around for a while, trying to chat to her, and stuff. He gave her some chocolate the other day. We just thought he was funny. He keeps staring at her with these great big puppy-dog eyes – like he's adoring her from a distance. Which is good, because I might kick him if he got much closer. But now he's written a song about her." Lark rolled her eyes. "He's in a band, apparently."

"A song?" Emily squeaked. That sounded quite cool. "Is it any good?"

Lark shrugged. "Look it up. He put it on YouTube."

Emily and Robin had raced home after that, desperate to see. They'd played the song on the laptop they shared for homework, hunched over the screen and giggling. Even though they had the volume down low, Lory had still heard, and thundered down the stairs and grabbed the laptop, slamming it shut after they'd heard just a few bars.

"Oi! That's ours!" Robin complained. "You can't stop us watching it. We'll just wait till you go out. Anyone who wants to can see it. Loads of people have already. It's got more than a thousand views. So I don't see why we can't look at it too."

"Because this is my house and I live here, and that song's about me, and he never asked if he could write me a stupid song!" Lory snarled,

marching back upstairs with the laptop under her arm.

"It sounded all right!" Emily called after her. "I quite liked it, that first bit. Why's it such a problem, anyway? You could be famous!"

"I don't want to be famous for having some floppy-haired fourteen-year-old write a song about me!" Lory yelled, flinging her arms out and then staring in horror as the laptop slid from her fingers.

Emily gasped, stretching out one hand in a hopeless catching sort of gesture. But Robin was suddenly, *magically*, there next to Lory, grabbing the computer in the split-second before it bounced fatally down the stairs.

"Be careful!" Emily cried.

Lory shuffled her feet on the stairs, and

muttered, "Sorry." Then she gulped, and ran off up to her room.

"Just because you're cross it doesn't mean you get to break our stuff!" Robin yelled after her. "And you can't stop us listening to that song either!"

Lory's bedroom door slammed shut so hard the stairs shook, and Robin went straight back to the table, opened the laptop and turned the volume up as high as he could.

"Are you trying to annoy her on purpose?" Lark had asked, wandering in from the kitchen, nibbling on a banana and shuddering as she heard the voice float out from the laptop, syrupy-sweet. "Ugh, turn it down. That song makes me feel sick."

Emily nodded. "I can see why Lory's cross. The first bit sounded OK, but now I can hear it

properly and he sounds like he's singing through about six spoonfuls of sugar. And the words aren't much better."

"I know." Lark sighed. "But that's not why she's cross."

Emily and Robin frowned at her.

"Why is she, then? She *said* it was a stupid song. . ." Robin asked, shrugging.

"She likes it." Lark slumped down on the sofa next to them. "She doesn't want to like it, but she's flattered, and sort of embarrassed at the same time. Loads of the girls at school were asking her about it today. They were all really jealous." She took a vicious bite of banana.

"Do you think she'll go out with him?" Emily asked, her eyes widening.

"I hope not," Lark muttered. "He makes my skin crawl." And she had stomped off upstairs and slammed her bedroom door even harder than Lory had.

Emily's room was on the floor above Lory's and she'd heard the song what felt like a few million times since then. Lory played it a lot. A few times Lark had come up Emily's rickety little staircase and curled up on Emily's window seat, staring gloomily out of the windows. She seemed a bit lost and in need of company. Emily loved it, having Lark to talk to. It made her feel older, and special. But at the same time it worried her, seeing her older sisters growing apart. And all because of a boy that none of them liked very much.

Now Emily leaned towards the kitchen door

and watched Lory flick her hair around and laugh as Dan said something funny. There was another rumbling growl from under the table.

Lark heard her twin giggling and hunched her shoulders irritably.

Emily sucked at her spoonful of cake scrapings and eyed Lark sideways. "Why does she suddenly like him now? She hated him a couple of weeks ago – when he wrote that song. She had a go at me and Robin for playing it."

Lark shivered. "I don't know. I really don't see why she lets him hang around. She used to say he made her feel sick. But now he's sitting with us every lunchtime out on the field. Him and his mates, who don't even say anything. They just laugh at his dumb jokes." Lark let her

spoon clatter into the bowl and put her chin in her hands.

Robin eagerly snatched the rest of the mixture for himself, but Lark didn't even seem to notice. Robin shot a worried glance at Emily.

"She does tell him to get lost sometimes, but she never sounds as if she means it all that much," Lark added. "And now he's coming to the house as well." She shivered again, shaking her soft brown hair forward so it covered her face as she hunched over. "I don't like him being here. . ."

3

After that, Dan Hargreaves seemed to be back every day, standing at the front door and chatting to Lory.

"Why doesn't he ever come in?" Emily asked Lory a few days later, after she'd closed the front door and wandered into the kitchen, smiling foolishly.

Lory looked at her in surprise, as though

she actually hadn't thought about it until now. "Well . . . I suppose I never asked him," she admitted. "And he never said he wanted to."

"Who never wanted to what?" their mother asked, coming past with an empty teacup and looking curiously at Lory. Their huge dog, Gruff, padded after her and nosed lovingly at Emily. He sniffed at Lory once and stepped back, his ears flattening. Emily scratched his chin and watched Lory trying to think what to say.

Lory flushed painfully scarlet, the colour rising up from her neck like a tide.

"There's a boy from school who likes her," Emily explained. Then she frowned. Dan had somehow managed to avoid meeting Eva or Ash. She nibbled one fingertip. That felt a bit

45

suspicious, a bit wrong. Was he avoiding them? And if so, why?

And more to the point, how? The house was surrounded by guard spells so strong and sensitive that Emily's dad could practically tell the postman's life history. Dan shouldn't have been able to sneak around without being noticed.

"Shut up, Emily," Lory muttered. "You're such a little busybody. It's nothing, Mum. Just ignore her." She hurried out of the kitchen and upstairs, leaving Eva and Emily staring after her.

"She's got a boyfriend?" Emily's mum asked, raising her eyebrows in perfect arches.

Emily shrugged. "No-oo. Maybe . . . I don't

think so. He likes her, Lark says. Lory wasn't so sure, but now she's always chatting to him. . . He wrote her a song, but it's terrible."

Eva nodded slowly. "A boy. . . Maybe he could come over for dinner. . . Your dad would *definitely* want to meet him." She sighed. "Yes. Dinner. Lovely. I'll get Lory to tell him."

"Mmm. Maybe. . ." But Emily was pretty sure Dan wouldn't come. She left her mum making more tea – Eva was designing a new fabric print, and that meant she drank bathtubs full of tea – and went upstairs. Lark and Lory both had their doors firmly closed and there was music coming from behind both of them. So they weren't in the same room, which was a bit worrying.

Before Dan Hargreaves had turned up, the sisters were always together, stretched out on each other's bedroom floors, gossiping or reading or singing along with the radio. It was as if Dan had planted himself in the middle, and now Lark and Lory couldn't see each other properly any more.

Suddenly cross, Emily banged on Robin's bedroom door and then flung it open.

"Watch it!" Robin cried. "You scared Brownie." He was lying on his front on his bed, peering into his cupped hands.

As Emily came closer, she saw that Robin was holding the tiny little chocolatey mouse. She giggled. Robin was also holding a chocolate digestive biscuit, which was about twice as big as the mouse was. It was melting. Both Robin and the mouse were staring up at her indignantly, and there was chocolate all over the mouse's great moustache of white whiskers.

"Is that what he's called? Brownie?" Emily asked, kneeling on the floor next to the bed and looking at the mouse. He glared back at her suspiciously and then went back to nibbling the chocolate digestive.

"Mm-hm. I thought it was a good name. And it fits. They're definitely his favourite food."

"Shouldn't he be eating normal mouse stuff?" Emily suggested. "Like, sunflower seeds? And peanuts?"

"He likes peanut butter fudge," said Robin.

"No! I mean just peanuts. I don't think mice are supposed to eat sweets."

49

"This one is." Robin shrugged slightly. "I did buy him some mouse food. I added it on to Mum's online shopping order without her noticing. Don't tell her about him, will you? She doesn't like mice."

"OK. Didn't he take to the mice food then?"

"No. He sulked until I gave him a bag of Maltesers *and* two of Dad's After Eights. Don't tell Dad either, by the way. He noticed the After Eights had gone."

"How did a mouse that small eat a whole bag of Maltesers?" Emily said, peering at Brownie. He was very tiny, but having said that, he was making good progress on the chocolate digestive. Slow but steady. He just had to keep stopping to suck chocolate off his whiskers.

"Well, I might have helped him a bit. And I had a couple of After Eights too. And I did have to give Gruff one, because he was being a bit jealous about Brownie. But Dad said half the box was gone and that just wasn't true. Anyway, he's a chocolate mouse, Ems. He's just made that way. And you were the one who made him, so you can't complain. In fact, I think it's your duty to help me feed him properly. Can you make us some brownies?"

Robin stared at her pleadingly and Emily was sure that the mouse had understood too. He stopped eating and his ears seemed to prick up. There was definitely an excited, hopeful look in his tiny, dark-chocolate eyes.

"I'll make some later, I promise. But I need

to talk to you about something important first."

Robin sat up, hugging Brownie against him tightly. The little mouse peered accusingly at Emily over the top of Robin's fingers. "What have you done now?" Robin whispered crossly. "Please tell me you haven't rescued another random water sprite? You're going to get me into so much trouble with Mum and Dad!"

"It's nothing like that!" Emily swallowed. "And it isn't my fault, this time, anyway. It's Lory. I'm worried about her."

Robin snorted. "Why? Lory can look after herself, Emily. Better than you can."

"It's that boy. None of us like him, have you noticed that? Lark really doesn't—"

52

"Because she's jealous! She's not used to Lory wanting to hang around with someone who isn't her."

"Maybe. But I don't think it's just that." Emily frowned. "He hasn't met Mum or Dad. They haven't even seen him out of the window, or anything like that. How come? Should he be able to do that?"

Robin looked at her seriously and Emily realized he was finally paying proper attention to what she was saying. "No. No, he shouldn't. Are you sure? Dad doesn't know anything about him?"

"Mum said he didn't. He'd have told her, wouldn't he?"

"I suppose so. . ."

"What does it mean?" Emily asked nervously. "Is Dan one of you?"

"No!" Robin laughed scornfully. "I'd be able to tell. Unless he had really amazing disguise spells. And Lory would know, wouldn't she? Don't be stupid."

Emily bit her lip to stop herself saying something grumpy back. She had a feeling that Robin was being so rude about it because he wasn't actually certain he was right. And he was scared.

"Can people do disguise spells like that?"

"Yes," Robin muttered. "But you have to be very strong. It's like when Lark and Lory were telling you about make-up, remember? You asked why didn't they just do it with magic, but it's not so

easy, because you have to keep the spell going for so long, and make sure it's the same every time someone sees you. Same for a disguise spell." He shook his head. "He really can't be one of us. I'm sure I'd know."

He didn't look very sure, though, and Brownie had stopped eating the biscuit, as if he could feel that something was wrong – although it could just have been that he was full. Emily reckoned he'd already eaten at least his own weight in digestive. The little mouse pattered down Robin's arm and on to the bedside table, where he crawled inside one of Eva's pretty painted teacups. Robin must have borrowed it from the kitchen. It was lined with what looked like a sock, and Brownie curled up in it blissfully.

"Do you think we should talk to Lark about it?" Emily suggested. "The thing is, she's already in a bad mood because she's missing Lory. . ."

Robin shook his head. "No. We ought to investigate. Next time he turns up, we'll spy on them."

"All right." It felt good to have a plan, even if it wasn't a very great one. Emily gave a little sigh of relief. "So. Normal brownies, or do you want white chocolate chips in them?"

Robin leaned back against his bedroom wall, frowning. "Don't mind. Whatever you like."

Which made Emily think he was really, really worried.

*

"He's here!" Robin came dashing out into the garden where Emily was sitting on the rocks at the edge of the pond, talking to Sasha.

"The boy?" Sasha asked curiously. Emily had told her about him. She looked hopefully at Robin. "Where are Lady Eva and Lord Ash?"

Emily blinked. It always took her a moment to work out who Sasha meant when she called their mum and dad that. She kept forgetting how important they were in the fairy world – that they were members of the royal court, even though they lived here.

"Both working." Robin said. "Emily's right. He only turns up when they're not going to see him. There's no way I'm interrupting Dad writing.

Someone phoned a bit earlier on and he did his evil dinosaur roar down the phone and then threw it at the door."

"And Mum said not to disturb her unless it was an emergency." Emily frowned anxiously.

"So . . . they're both busy? I could come inside and see him?" Sasha suggested.

Robin looked at her in surprise. "What for?"

"Well, if he's someone from our world, there's a chance I might recognize him," Sasha said humbly.

"Yes!" Emily squeaked eagerly. "Come on. But no one can see you. Lark and Lory don't know about you either, and I don't want either of them finding out. They'd probably blackmail me – make me tidy their rooms or something."

"OK, but if they see her, or Mum or Dad do, I didn't know anything, all right?" Robin stood blocking the kitchen doorway, staring grimly at Emily.

"All right! But they won't. We'll be careful. Really, really careful, I promise."

"I could transform," Sasha whispered as they tiptoed into the kitchen.

"Into what?" Emily asked, fascinated.

Sasha shrugged. "Water would be easiest."

"You can turn into water?"

"Of course – I'm a water fairy." Sasha smiled at her, but Robin shook his head.

"No. For a start using too much magic round here means Mum or Dad will notice. We were lucky with Emily's spell to make Brownie." A

59

small dark head appeared over the collar of Robin's thin cotton shirt – the mouse had heard his name. "No, no food. Go back to sleep. And anyway, how much water are we talking about? We're not carrying you around in a bucket – that's going to look really obvious. And what if we spill you?"

Sasha's eyes widened. "Perhaps not. Although it can be useful. Especially if I have to hide."

Emily giggled. "There'd just be this strange puddle. . . But for the minute, let's just try and keep you hidden in your girl form."

They peered round the kitchen door, looking in the hallway and trying to listen for Lory and the boy.

"I reckon they've gone upstairs," Robin muttered,

edging out into the hallway, and frowning up at the stairs above them. "She's actually brought him into the house this time. And none of the guard spells noticed – or at least Dad didn't come storming out of his study."

"So maybe he is just an ordinary boy," Emily said, frowning. "If he was a fairy like you, surely that would have triggered the spells?"

"Dad knows even if it's humans in the house," Robin pointed out. "He has to be really careful, because of the doors. Dad ought to know that Dan's here, whoever he is. I don't think he's human at all. Come on. We'd better go and see where they are."

The three of them went creeping up the stairs. It felt like a game of hide and seek, and Emily

wanted to giggle. But Sasha was following close behind her, her hand wound into Emily's, and she was trembling, Emily could feel it.

"Are you sure you want to do this?" Emily whispered. "You're shaking."

"I want to help," Sasha murmured back. "I like your sisters. And Lark was crying yesterday. She sat by the pond and some of her tears fell in the water. I could feel them – I could feel her. She doesn't suspect Dan's anything other than a boy, but she doesn't trust him either. And she misses her twin."

Emily nodded, hating the thought of Lark crying.

"And if this Dan is only using Lory to get through one of the doors, who knows what'll

happen to her? What if he takes her with him?" Sasha shook her greenish hair and shivered.

Robin stopped dead and Emily bumped into him. He looked round at Sasha, his eyes suddenly a stormy grey and his lips pale. "Is that what you think he's trying to do?"

Sasha shrugged gracefully, the watery fabric of her dress shimmering over her shoulders. "I don't know. Maybe not. Maybe he's just any old boy. But that's what it sounds like, doesn't it?"

"I was hoping it didn't," Robin muttered. "They must be in her room with the door shut. I can't hear them, can you?"

Emily shook her head. "No. So one of us is going to have to knock and ask something."

"Not me!" Robin grabbed hold of the banister and Emily stared at him.

"What are you doing that for?"

"I'm touching wood."

"So?" Emily folded her arms.

"So you have to do the knocking?" Robin said, hopefully.

"Since when does touching wood mean that!"

Robin frowned. "It does mean something, though, doesn't it? Anyway, I called it. Bagsy not me, touching wood, pinch, punch, first of the month. Whatever. You're doing it."

"Fine!" Emily whispered back, rolling her eyes, and she marched across the landing. "Sasha, if you stand over there, just by Robin's manky tip of a bedroom, you should be able

64

to see into Lory's room when she opens the door."

Sasha seemed to flow over the wooden boards of the landing, and when she pressed herself against the wall, Emily had to blink to be able to see her again. She was practically invisible – just a thin, watery shape against the grubby paintwork.

Emily nodded at her, and then banged loudly on Lory's door. She was expecting Lory to yell at her to go away, but there was only silence. And not the kind of silence when the people inside the room are just hoping that whoever's knocking will just go away.

"Where are they?" Robin hissed. "Where's she taken him?"

65

"Well, they aren't going to be in Lark's room," Emily muttered. "They weren't anywhere downstairs. . . Check Mum and Dad's bedroom."

Robin hurried off down the short passage from the landing to their parents' room, and Emily ran quickly up the little staircase to her own room in the attic, her heart going in sickening thumps. The thought of that strange boy being up there in her lovely bedroom made the hairs stand up all over her arms. Lory wouldn't have done that, would she? Not without asking? But then . . . she seemed different now. Not as nice.

Robin came back shaking his head. "Nope. No one there."

"What's through there?" Sasha asked. She was

66

still semi-transparent and her voice seemed to come out of nowhere.

Emily jumped. She had walked right past the water fairy. Her disguise was so good that Emily had almost forgotten she was there. "Where?"

"That door. I think I can hear voices coming from behind it too."

"There isn't a door," Emily started to say, looking where Sasha was looking. But there was.

She should have been used to it by now. The house was full of doors that moved and changed colour, and occasionally disappeared entirely. For years, Emily had told herself that it was her imagination, or just a trick of the light, because after all, it couldn't be anything else, could it? And none of them had ever opened, not for her.

She stared grimly at this door now. It was small and dark, and actually very hard to see. It gave off a strong sense of not being there at all – as if it was shy. The handle was tiny – and as Emily looked at it, a shadow seemed to fall across the door, so that she couldn't see the handle at all. "I know it's there," she hissed, and grabbed it.

"What are you two doing?" someone asked, behind them. "And who's *she*?"

4

Emily let go of the door and whirled round, staring at Lark in horror. "No one. . ." she said, crossing her fingers behind her back and hoping that Lark would somehow believe her. After all, *she* could hardly see Sasha.

"Don't be stupid," her older sister snapped. "Are you a water fairy? Where on earth did you come from?"

Sasha had practically disappeared under Robin's bedroom door. She had told Emily she could turn to water, but Emily hadn't really believed her, until she saw it happening. The silvery droplets trickled along the floorboards and shimmered softly as they grew upwards, transforming back into a tall, slim girl with weed-green hair. She leaned against the door frame and stared at Lark.

"You!" Lark came closer, peering at Sasha's face. "I *know* you! You were the one who showed us the door to get home, when we rescued Emily."

"And then they sent the hunters after her," Emily said, grabbing Lark's arm. Her sister's skin glittered and prickled under her fingers. "I know I shouldn't have done it, but I couldn't leave her there, Lark! They had dogs!"

"*You* brought her back?" Lark stared at her in disbelief.

"She can do all sorts of stuff, Lark," Robin put in.

"But she isn't. . ." Lark shrugged, and looked apologetically at Emily. "I don't mean this the way it sounds – but you aren't one of us, Emily. You shouldn't be able to do magic."

Lark didn't believe them, Emily could tell. "Show her the mouse," Emily said, and her voice was sharp. She was sick of everyone treating her like she was the useless one. She hadn't asked for any of this, and she wasn't making it up, either!

Robin reached into his shirt pocket and lifted out Brownie, waving him at Lark. The tiny mouse shook his whiskers grumpily and glared at her.

71

He'd obviously been asleep and he wasn't that happy about being woken up. His tail twitched and Lark took a step back. She didn't like mice, Emily realized, smiling to herself.

"What has . . . that . . . got to do with anything?" Lark muttered, putting her hands behind her back.

"Emily made him," Robin said triumphantly. "Out of a chocolate brownie. So there – so much for her not having any magic!"

"You turned a chocolate brownie into a mouse?" Lark shook her head at Emily. "Well, that was a waste, for a start. . . *How*?"

"I was actually trying to turn it into a cake. It went a bit wrong," Emily admitted. "But Robin and Sasha said that the way you all do magic isn't,

um, exact. I mean, there aren't magic words and spells you really have to learn, are there? You just make the magic happen. That's what I did, I think. Almost. And it was the same with bringing Sasha here. I wanted to, so I just did it."

"You just did it. . ." Lark echoed faintly.

"It isn't all that strange," Robin said. "She's been living in this house for ten years, after all. Every time one of the doors opens, magic seeps out, doesn't it? Emily's been through the doors, too, now. The magic's leaked into her."

"That makes me sound like some sort of experiment gone wrong," Emily said crossly.

"You are," Lark murmured. "That's the thing. There's never been a human child like you before, brought up in a house full of fairies,

exposed to who knows how much magic. No one knows how you'll turn out." She sighed and sat down on the bottom step of the stairs up to Emily's room. "This is turning into a really horrible day," she muttered.

"Thanks!" Emily blinked hard, feeling tears burning her eyes.

Lark reached out and grabbed her hand, pulling her down to sit. Then she wrapped an arm round Emily's shoulders.

"Are you putting some sort of spell on me?" Emily asked suspiciously. She could feel Lark's magic fluttering around her, feathery-light and loving.

"Not on purpose," Lark assured her. "It just happens, because I want to make you feel better.

I didn't mean to sound nasty. It's just – so much weird stuff is happening."

"Mmmm, like how Lory's up in the hidden attic with that boy right now," Robin said mock-casually.

"What?" Lark's head snapped round. "She took him up there?"

"Mm-hm."

"But it's full of secrets! It's got a disappearing door. How did she explain that?"

"We don't know! We were about to go and see when you started making a stupid fuss," Robin cried.

"What secrets?" Emily asked curiously. "What attic? I thought my bedroom was the attic." Then she stared down at her feet. "Am I allowed to

75

see?" she added, her tongue suddenly feeling swollen with shyness.

"If Lory's showing Dan Hargreaves, I don't see why we can't take you up there." Lark smiled. "It's just an attic, Ems, to be honest. Your room's on one side, and the attic runs along the back of the house. You must have realized your room wasn't the whole roof space."

Emily shook her head. "I never thought about it."

Lark shrugged. "Mmmm. Well. It's hidden. People who don't already know probably aren't supposed to think about it. It's an attic, that's all. You know, full of stuff we don't use much – old clothes, books, that sort of thing. But if you think about it, our old junk is a bit different to everyone else's."

Emily nodded slowly, imagining piles of ancient, crumbling books on spells and herbs and elvenlore, and trunks full of glittering clothes, and shoes that could dance by themselves. "Can we go and see?" she asked hopefully. "Can I have a look around up there?"

"Maybe when we've got rid of that boy. . ." Lark muttered. "I can't believe she let him see it. I suppose he won't really understand what it all is. He might not be able to see some of the stuff. But still, she must be mad."

"Or bewitched," Robin said, in a doom-laden voice.

"Oh, don't be silly. . ." But Lark sounded almost as worried as he did. Then she sprang up, staring at the little dark door. It seemed to

change as she held out one hand and looked at it. Emily saw it clearly for the first time. It was small and made of dark wood, carved in one long, strange, curling pattern, full of flowers and leaves and tiny birds.

"They're coming down," Lark murmured, raising her hand up now, pressing her palm towards the door, as if she wanted to ward something off. "You. . ." she looked round at Sasha. "I'm sorry, I don't know your name, and it isn't the time. Hide, please. We don't know what Dan is but he mustn't see you. You can't pass as human. We'd never be able to explain you away."

Sasha nodded, and swirled across the floor to the stairs up to Emily's room. Her dress swept Emily's face as she hurried past, leaving a suggestion of

dampness, and fresh water. Emily touched her fingers to her cheek and seemed to feel a stream running past, carrying things on.

Sasha hovered on the stairs behind them as a slight glimmer, just out of sight from the landing, and Emily turned back towards the door. Now she could hear them coming too – Lory's high, happy voice, and the lower tones of the boy. His voice seemed to wrap round Lory's, and even hearing him made Emily's hair tingle with dislike.

The door suddenly shone all over and Emily realized that Lory must have put her hand on it from the other side. Emily ducked back against Lark, peeping at the blazing doorway from behind her sister's shoulder.

The figures that came through it were fiery too. Lory in front, wrapped in a glorious light that seemed to echo the shape of her wings, even though she was still in her human form. Her eyes were glowing. The boy behind her was just as bright, the air around him swirling with a cold greenish mist that melted into the soft pink and crimson lights of Lory. The colours fought against each other, melding to a muddy, sickening brownish-purple at the edges – like a bruise, Emily thought. They were dangerous together. Lory must not have realized. Surely, if she could see the lights as Emily could, she'd send Dan away?

"He is one of you, I'm sure he must be," she whispered to Lark, who nodded, and hugged her tighter.

"Oh! Hello." Lory saw them – Emily and Lark on the step and Robin lurking by his bedroom door – and stopped, half out of the attic door, looking uncomfortable. The colours faded from both of them immediately and Dan shut the door behind him with a delicate click. He was smirking and Emily hated him.

"Hello," Lark said flatly. "We wondered where you were."

"Well, now you know." Lory's voice was brittle. Much harsher than usual. She darted one sharp, angry glare at her sister, and then she marched across the landing to the stairs, resolutely staring straight ahead.

Lark and Emily and Robin watched silently as they disappeared down the stairs. Emily felt she

couldn't even breathe until she heard the front door bang. Then she let out a long, shaky sigh.

"She went with him," Robin reported, leaning over the banisters. "They've both gone." He came back and crouched in front of the girls. "So, did you recognize him?" he asked, looking at Sasha.

"Yes." She was sitting behind Emily and Lark now, hunched up, with her arms wrapped round her middle as though she was hurting.

"What's the matter?" Emily asked, reaching out to stroke her arm. "You look awful! Who is he? Is he horrible?"

"I don't know exactly who he is," Sasha whispered. "But he is from our world. Most definitely. Looking at him burned. There was

something so icy, and . . . and stone-like about him. He's hard."

Emily nodded. "I saw it too. A sort of cold green light."

"It made him look different," Lark murmured. "Older, didn't you think? And familiar, somehow. Ohhh!" She curled her fingers into fists, frowning. "Why didn't we see it before? I can't believe we thought he was just some boy. I'm sure I do know him. I don't understand how he's managed to disguise himself from us all this time. And even from Lory. He has to be strong."

"I felt like I knew him too. Or maybe he only looks like someone we know," Robin suggested. "Like he's someone's brother."

"That's it!" Emily yelped, jumping so suddenly

she almost knocked Lark over. "He looks like Lady Anstis! That's why I didn't like him. He's a fair-haired version of her. He has to be related to her." She shivered. "What's he doing here, in disguise?"

"Are you sure? I didn't even know she had a brother," Lark said. "They're a very powerful family but I thought it was just her and her sisters."

"I'm almost sure," Emily murmured. "It's something about his eyes, and the way his eyebrows go up at the ends. I wish I'd noticed it before. He shouldn't be here, though, should he? Whoever he is? Not in disguise?"

"Nope." Robin shook his head so hard that his hair flapped and then settled round his head

again like dark-red feathers. "He's either sneaked through a secret door somewhere, not one of the proper ones, or he was exiled. But I thought if you were exiled they took away all of your powers first?" he added to Sasha and Lark, frowning.

"Maybe they did. . ." Sasha said. "Lady Anstis is very old, isn't she? Old enough that if he is her brother, he might well have been out here a very long time. Perhaps he's been building his powers back up. Lurking around the places where the magic leaks through. Like here. Maybe the old doors under the hills. Fairy rings."

"So. . ." Emily's voice was croaky with fear and she coughed a little. "So, he's an exiled fairy lord in disguise. What does he want with Lory?"

85

"We have to tell Lory." Lark sighed.

"She won't believe you," Robin pointed out.

"I know!" Lark snapped back. "You'll have to back me up."

"Won't that just make her cross though?" Emily suggested. "She might get annoyed if she thinks everyone knows he lied to her."

"Probably." Lark nodded gloomily. "But she saw us all here. She knows you saw him. And at least

she isn't going to think that you two are only jealous because she's got a boyfriend."

Emily and the others were silent for a minute. "Is that what she thinks you are?" Emily said cautiously.

"Mmmm. And before you ask, maybe I was a bit." Then Lark snorted. "But I wasn't just being jealous, was I? I was right. He *is* a creep. She should have listened to me to begin with."

Emily smiled, but she made up her mind to do as much of the talking as possible, if Lory would let her speak. Lark did sound a bit too gleeful, and Lory was so touchy.

"Should we tell Mum and Dad about who Dan really is?" Emily asked. "I mean, if he's really powerful and dangerous—"

"Don't you dare!" Lark said, suddenly angry. "If we do that Lory's never going to talk to me again. Really!" She caught Emily's wrist. "Please, Emily, I mean it. She's already going to be so miserable about it. And furious. We have to sort it out without Mum and Dad knowing. You know how proud she is. She'd hate it if they knew she'd been tricked like this."

"All right!" Emily shrugged, and pulled away. Lark knew more about this sort of thing than she did, after all. "I was only trying to help."

"I know." Lark rubbed her cheek against Emily's hair.

Lark was proud too, Emily thought. Too proud just to say sorry.

*

"Where did she go?" Robin muttered, walking up and down the back of the sofa, and kicking at the cushions. "She's been ages. I hate waiting." He and Emily and Lark were killing time waiting for Lory to get home. Sasha had gone back to the pond – she couldn't stay away from water for too long.

"We know," Emily sighed, leaning forward to dodge his feet, and grabbing some more popcorn while she happened to be close to the bowl. They were watching one of Lark's DVDs, a slushy sort of high school comedy, and it called for popcorn.

"She's coming." Lark had been slumped back against the end of the sofa, with her feet stretched out on Emily's lap. But now she sprang upright,

curling her feet under her with perfect, inhuman grace.

Emily moved up next to Robin, who had slipped down amongst the cushions. They weren't quite touching, but they were close enough that Emily could feel the warmth of him. She hated it when Lark and Lory fought. It happened so rarely that it frightened her. She could remember hating it always, a long time before she knew about their magic and what they could do to each other if they really tried. When Lark and Lory did anything more than tease each other, she and Robin would often find an excuse to be together. Once Emily remembered hiding with him under the kitchen table – it was less scary hearing Lark and Lory screeching at each

other when they could only see their sisters' feet.

Lark sat frowning in the corner of the sofa, listening to the steps coming up the path and the front door banging. Then, as Lory began to pad along the hallway, Lark stretched out a hand and twirled her fingers lightly in the air.

As she drew her hand away, a soft, speckled-brown feather appeared, tiny and fluffed at the root. It floated upwards, wafting out across the room, drawn by invisible, unnatural air currents that sent it skimming into the hall.

Lory's soft footsteps halted. A moment later she appeared in the doorway of the living room, the feather cupped in her hands.

"What?" she asked mulishly. "I'm tired. I'm going upstairs."

91

"We need to talk to you first." Lark hesitated, and Emily held her breath.

"Hurry up, then!"

"It's Dan."

Lory rolled her eyes, but Lark galloped on. "Please listen," she begged. "It isn't just me being weird about him. Emily and Robin saw it too."

They nodded and Lory scowled. "Saw what?"

"He's one of us," Lark told her simply.

Lory stared at Lark and then shrugged impatiently. "You think I didn't know that?"

All three of them gaped at her, speechless, and Lory laughed. "You look so funny. Like three fish."

"You *knew*?" Lark asked, her voice hollow with disbelief.

"Of course. He told me." Lory smiled shyly and

her eyes unfocused a little, as though she was remembering. "Not at first. He had to make sure that he could trust me. But now he does."

"He's an exile?" Robin asked.

Lory nodded, her eyes still misty. "It was all a mistake – he was trying to convince the king not to be so harsh towards some of the lesser peoples. The forest fairies. He was protecting them. But the king thought Dantis was trying to usurp the throne, so he exiled him."

"Dantis sounds a lot like Anstis," Robin whispered to Emily. "I think you were right."

Lark was still gaping at her sister. "But – but you didn't tell me," she murmured.

Lory looked uncomfortable for the first time. "I wanted to," she admitted. "Dan said it was too

risky." She looked at Lark under her eyelashes. "He doesn't think you like him."

"I don't!" Lark snapped. "I think he's lying to you."

"Oh, don't be so stupid!" Lory whirled round, ready to stomp away, but the feather squashed in between her fingers twisted again. "*What?*"

"Please listen." Lark swallowed and spoke slowly, picking her words carefully. "It was when we saw him come down out of the attic with you. He looked wrong, we all thought so. I think he's dangerous."

"What does he want?" Robin added, and both sisters jumped, as though they'd almost forgotten anyone else was there.

Lory hesitated. She didn't really want to answer, Emily could see. "A door," she admitted at last.

"You see! He's using you!" Lark jumped up from the sofa. "He just wants you to get him back – it's all a lie."

"No, it isn't!" Lory shrieked. For a horrible moment, her face sharpened in a way that reminded Emily of Lady Anstis. She looked fierce and angry and knowing. And then her face crumpled, as if she wasn't truly sure, and she was just their sister again. "He really does like me," she muttered.

"You can't let him through any of the doors," Lark told her pleadingly. "You mustn't. We're forbidden."

"I'm not going to. I can't. They're all guarded." Lory shrugged. "But Dantis thinks there's another door, a hidden one. He says it's here

95

somewhere. We're looking for it, together. And then I'm going to help him return and overthrow the tyranny."

Lark raised her eyebrows. "You do know that's just another way of saying that you're going to kill the king? Our king? He's even related to us, Lory – he's like some kind of distant great-uncle!"

"He's an oppressor," Lory said, but she sounded like a little child, parroting something she had been taught. "He rules the people too harshly."

Lark frowned. "How do you even know? We've never lived there. You don't know, not for certain. Only what he's telling you, don't you see? And how do you know that Dantis would be any better?"

"Especially if he's related to Lady Anstis and

her sisters," Emily put in. "He looks so like her, Lory. I think he's her brother."

"Dantis and Anstis," Robin agreed. "They sound the same. He might even be worse than she is."

Lory stared at him, and then at Emily. "Anstis – the one we rescued you from?" She shook her head, slowly. "No. No, he would have told me. I'm sure he isn't."

"Just think of him with darker hair," Emily reminded her. "And jewelled clothes instead of school uniform or a T-shirt."

Lory shook her head again, stubbornly, but Emily could see she was troubled. Unfortunately Lory hated to be confused, or uncertain. It made her angry. Her eyebrows had drawn together,

Emily saw now, and her lips were tightly stretched and very pale.

"I should have known you'd be like this," she hissed. "So stupid and petty."

"Petty! We're trying to stop you breaking the most important rule our family has!" Lark yelled. "You can't take him through the doors, and it doesn't matter if it's a secret one somewhere – it's still in this house. It's still up to Dad to guard it. You're putting us all in danger. I'm going to tell Dad."

"No!" Lory bounded forward, screaming it in Lark's face. "You won't! I won't let you." She still had the feather, nestled in her fingers, and she dropped back a step, breathing on it, oh so gently. Her eyes were glowing with an angry amber light.

A wisp of pale blue smoke rose from the feather, and a sizzling noise, and the most dreadful smell of burning.

Lark staggered back as though the feather had been a part of her. Emily grabbed at her, worrying that she was going to fall, but let go with a yelp – Lark felt as though she was burning too.

Robin stood between the sisters, his eyes flicking frantically from Lark to Lory, his hands lifted as if he wanted to stop them – but he couldn't tell how.

"Don't do that to her!" Emily yelled at Lory. "You're hurting her, stop it!"

"I won't let her betray us," Lory snarled, but she was crying, tears running down her face in little glittering streams. She stroked the frizzled

remnants of the feather across her cheek, and Lark sighed, sinking down to the floor with her arms wrapped round her middle.

"What did you do?" Emily wailed, crouching next to Lark. "How could you do that to her? She's your sister!"

"I stopped it, I mended her," Lory muttered, holding out the feather, which was whole again now, although bleached white. It was shaking on Lory's palm, although it was actually Lory shaking, Emily realized after a moment. She was trembling all over and there were still tears pouring down her face. "But if you tell Mum and Dad, it will burn again, Lark, you know it will. We're bound together by our magic, you and me. You can't betray me."

Emily shook her head, disbelieving. She'd seen Lory angry, in a temper. She'd known her to scream at Lark, but the sisters had never hurt each other, not like this. It was new – and wrong.

Lark stood up, wavering a little, with Emily holding her. "You can't take Dantis through the doors," she murmured. "I may not be able to tell Dad, but I'll stop you myself." She was crying too. Emily could feel her gasps. "Doesn't it matter to you that we're all frightened? We don't trust him – it's *you* we're frightened for!"

"You just don't understand." Lory shook her head. She looked miserable but determined. Horribly certain. "I have to do it."

"No!" Lark yelled, suddenly tearing herself out of Emily's arms and springing at her sister.

Emily reached out a hand helplessly, wanting to pull her back.

Lark and Lory were standing face to face, Lory still cupping the feather in her hands, a grim look on her face. Lark had lifted her hands up to her shoulders, as though she was calling something down, and her dress was swirling around her legs with the rising wind. The wind spun around the room, fluttering and tearing, and Robin caught Emily's hand.

"What's she doing?" Emily wailed.

"I don't know. But why haven't Mum or Dad noticed?" Robin took a step towards his sisters. "Lark and Lory aren't strong enough to hide all this magic from them. They should know! Why aren't they here stopping them?"

Emily shook her head. "Something's hiding the magic? I don't know either!"

The magic that Lark was calling flared, sending a sudden gust of air at Lory, air laden with power, like a thunderstorm. Little sparks of lightning ran through it, but Lory simply smiled and held out the feather, which began to shrivel and burn in the surge of Lark's own fiery magic.

Lark dropped back, coughing and gasping, and dark, dreadful marks appeared on the thin cotton of her dress. Burn marks.

"I think she's actually going to burn up!" Emily cried. "This isn't Lory doing this, she never would. Not to Lark!" She darted across the room, reaching for a vase of flowers on a shelf, hopelessly planning

103

to tip the water over Lark. But would water put out a fire spell?

"Let me." Sasha was swinging herself in through the open window. She was half water already, shadowy and thin and shining, and she wrapped herself around the squirming Lark with soft murmurs of comfort.

"A water sprite?" Lory muttered. Then she looked down at the feather again, whole, but terribly, wispily fragile. She closed it in her hand, squeezing angrily, and stalked away.

6

"Help me take her out into the garden," Sasha panted. "She's still burning up inside. I need to be nearer water to help her."

Emily and Robin stood on either side of Lark, holding her limp arms around their shoulders, while Sasha walked in front. She had stretched out her dress like a sheet of watery magic and

wrapped it around herself and Lark, pulling her gently out towards the garden.

Lark could walk, but she was stumbling and weak, and her face was anguished. Emily couldn't tell if that was because of the burning spell, or because it was Lory who had cast it against her.

They had just reached the pond – and Emily and Robin were crouching, helping Lark to sit among the reeds around the pond so Sasha could be in the water and still reach her – when Emily caught a movement out of the corner of her eye. She looked round, and then quickly slipped out from under Lark's arm. "It's Rachel," she whispered to Robin. "She said she might come round today. I forgot. I have to stop her walking over here."

"Hello!" Rachel, Emily's best friend from school, came round the corner of the house, waving. "Isn't it hot? Want to go and buy an ice cream from the shop?"

Emily glanced back quickly and Robin nodded, shooing her away. He turned and stooped forward so that if Rachel looked over, she wouldn't see Sasha.

Lark was stronger already, Emily thought gratefully. She wasn't slumped over any more – now she was strong enough to stretch out her hand to Sasha in the water.

"Yes. Um. Yes, ice cream sounds good." Actually, it sounded wonderful. She still felt as though she was burning a little, just from touching Lark. It made her shiver to think what Lark must feel like.

She reached out to take Rachel's arm, wanting to lead her away from the scene in the garden as quickly as she could. But Rachel jumped back, staring at her in surprise.

"Emily, your fingers are burning! Wow, have you been sitting in the sun for ages or something?"

"Oh . . . yes." Emily snatched her hand away. "Sorry."

Rachel gazed at her, head on one side, frowning a little. "You look odd. . ."

"Too much sun?" Emily smiled, trying to shrug it off. Was it any wonder she looked strange?

"No. You're . . . glittering." Rachel was staring at Emily's hands, and Emily glanced down at them, wondering what she meant.

"Oh!" She was. A thin sheen of greenish-silver

water magic slid over her fingers as she held them out. It had dripped on to her when Sasha was trying to soothe Lark, Emily supposed. Swiftly, Emily stuck her hands behind her back and smiled. "I was painting," she lied. "Earlier on. Nice colour, isn't it? I didn't know I'd got it all over me though." She pulled a tissue out of the pocket of her shorts and rubbed it furiously over her hands, muttering in her head, *Go away, go away, go away* . . . and trying to will her fingers clean and pinkish again.

It was all about wishing Sasha and Robin had said. Not rhyming spells, or newts' eyes, or anything like that. She just had to take the magic inside her and *need* it. She couldn't let Rachel know the truth – it was too dangerous, for everybody.

Emily's hands itched and prickled as she

scrubbed, and there was a very, very faint buzzing sound. When she stretched her fingers out again, they were clean, but with that odd tight feeling – the kind she got after she'd been washing up in water that was hotter than it should have been.

"Glittery paint?" Rachel asked. She sounded a little too interested and Emily remembered how much she liked sparkly things – glittery nail polish especially.

"Mmm. It's new. Belongs to Mum, really," Emily added quickly, in case Rachel wanted to see it.

"Oh." Rachel nodded enviously. Emily's mum, being a dress designer, had a whole cupboard full of fabric scraps and beads and buttons as well as the most amazing art supplies.

Emily hurried her friend down the path towards the gate and the street, wishing she could tell Rachel what was really happening. She had told Rachel that she'd found out she was adopted, but not the whole truth about her family. She wished she could – Rachel was her best friend and she hated hiding stuff from her. And it would be so nice to show her a spell . . . once she was a bit better at them. She couldn't though. Emily understood why her mum had made her promise. The knowledge would put their whole family in danger, and Rachel too.

"I could really do with an ice cream," she chattered. "It's so hot, isn't it? Shall we go and eat them under the trees in the park?"

It was nice to be away from the house for

a bit, Emily thought, as she buried her tingly hands in the ice cream freezer at the newsagent. She was going to have to go back quite soon and make sure Lark was all right, of course, but she needed some time to . . . to be normal. Which was funny, because usually she didn't like being normal at all.

What would she have been like if she had grown up with her real family, Emily wondered as they lay under the big willow tree in the park and she stared at the leaves, flickering above her.

Her father had found her under a willow tree, so he'd told her. Wrapped in a blanket and laughing up at the leaves waving over her head. Maybe that was why she liked the long fronds

of the willows so much. They still made her feel peaceful.

She couldn't have minded being left, Emily thought, rather sadly. She didn't think about her real parents that often – she'd had too much else to think about, to be honest – but just sometimes, the fact that she was adopted would hit her all over again.

Actually, she wasn't adopted, officially. Ash and Eva had simply pretended that she was theirs. Emily suspected it wasn't difficult to do that sort of thing when you could just pull spells out of the air and use them to make people believe whatever you wanted.

"I'm going to have to go home," Rachel said, rolling over with a sigh. "I told Mum I'd be back in

an hour. She watches the clock. I swear she still thinks I'm too little to go anywhere without her."

"It's because you're an only child," Emily said as she sat up. "One of the few good things about big sisters. . ." She shivered as she said it, remembering all at once just what her big sisters had been doing. "They've always done everything before you have. I'd have to try really hard to scare my mum."

"I know, your mum's so relaxed compared to mine." Rachel shrugged. "OK. This is it. I'm actually getting up."

She didn't, but Emily reached down and hauled her up from the grass. Now she'd thought about Lark and Lory, she knew she had to go home.

*

"Oh! Hi, Mum." Emily pulled up in surprise as she came into the kitchen. She'd expected her mother to be stuck in her studio all day, but she was sitting at the kitchen table, with her fingers twisted together. She didn't look happy.

And her dad was by the sink, she noticed then, filling the kettle. He didn't look happy either – positively grim, in fact.

Emily chewed the inside of her bottom lip, wondering what they knew. Had they heard Lark and Lory fighting? Or come across traces of magic, left over from the battle between her sisters?

Or perhaps – Emily swallowed back a horrified gulp – perhaps Lark had been really hurt by Lory's magic and Robin had to call them to help her?

What about the secrecy spell that Lory had laid on Lark? Would it still have attacked her if Robin was the one who told?

Emily suspected her parents didn't know what had really happened between Lark and Lory. If they did, they'd be with Lark, wouldn't they? Not sitting in the kitchen, making tea and glaring at her. None of it had been her fault, Emily thought uneasily. Why did they look as though it was her they were cross with?

"Er, what's the matter?" she asked at last.

"Don't you know?" her father snapped.

Emily shook her head slowly. She glanced sideways and saw that Robin was standing by the open door to the garden. He smiled at her and made a little thumbs up sign towards the garden.

So Lark was all right then! Emily nodded and then rolled her eyes anxiously at him. What was going on?

"Did you know about this?" Eva asked him, her voice shaking a little.

"What?" Robin opened his eyes impossibly wide as he strolled over to stand by Emily. His dark lashes quivered innocently and his mother sighed. Even though she knew it was all put on, the look still worked.

"The nixie," she said, frowning at Emily.

Emily only stared back at her. She had no idea what a nixie was.

"Water sprite," Robin muttered out of the corner of his mouth.

Oh! Sasha!

Emily hadn't even considered that... She actually was the one in trouble, then.

"In the pond!" their father added, his voice almost a growl.

Emily bit her lip again, but this time to stop herself laughing. It was the way he'd said it. As though it didn't matter that she'd done the most forbidden thing and brought a fairy creature through the doors and into the human world. The problem was that she'd put her in the garden pond.

"She – um – needed the water," she said, her voice wobbling a little as she tried not to smirk.

"She needs to be where she belongs!" her father yelled. "What were you doing? You promised never to go back without one of us! I explained to

118

you how dangerous it was. And then you actually brought someone through!"

"I still don't think it can have been Emily," Eva said wearily. "It doesn't make sense. Lory must have got mixed up, Ash. Emily couldn't have done it."

"Lory!" Robin whispered, just as Emily glanced at him and hissed, "Lory told them!"

He nodded. "Good way to keep them off her tracks. Get them worried about you instead."

"I take it you *did* know," Ash glowered at Robin, "going by the whispering. Was it you that brought her over?" He sank into a chair next to Eva. "You're right, it must have been Robin. Emily couldn't, of course. Silly of me."

"It *was* me!" Emily said, her eyes filling with

tears. It was stupid to be disappointed that they were cross with someone else instead of her, but Emily was proud of what she'd done, rescuing Sasha. Yes, she'd promised her parents she wouldn't go back to the fairy world, but some things were more important even than promises, weren't they?

But her parents were smiling at her sadly, as though they thought she was sweet and a bit stupid. Emily smacked the table with her open hand. "It was!"

"It was Emily that brought me here," a quiet voice added, in the second's silence after the mugs stopped shaking. Everyone turned towards the door.

The kitchen was dim and shadowed against the

bright sunlight in the garden, and it was hard to see Sasha standing there – just the faint outline of a girl and the scent of water.

"And you aren't sending her back," Emily hissed at her father. "I won't let you. Don't you see, if she goes back she'll die."

"What?" Eva turned back and stared at Emily. "What are you talking about?"

"I'm being hunted." Sasha drifted slowly closer, lurking warily just behind Emily.

"That may be so – but you should not be here, water-girl," Ash said, his voice deep and sad.

Emily gripped Sasha's hand. She couldn't let this happen. But her father had told her so firmly – no one was ever to come through the doors without permission. Whatever the reason.

And he was angry with Sasha now. And with her too. What if he sent Sasha back? Emily knew he could, easily.

"She helped us escape from Lady Anstis. I had to help her." Emily caught her breath and stepped closer to her father, pushing Sasha back towards Robin. "I know I'm not meant to have any magic, but I have, because *you* brought me here. That's how I went through to the fairy world in the first place, *and* how I brought Sasha back!" She glared at him. "And even if I didn't have any magic, I'd still have wanted to help her. I don't care about your rules! She was going to die!"

Eva reached out suddenly and caught Emily's hand, pulling her close. Emily squeaked in surprise, but her mother took her other hand

122

too, clasping them tightly in her own. She closed her eyes, the great fans of dark lashes fluttering against her cheeks. Then she began to whisper, in a language Emily didn't know. She didn't know it, but she recognized it. Her mother had sung those words to her before, she remembered. When she was tiny and wouldn't go to sleep. Emily could feel the love and magic in them, and in the trembling of her mother's voice as she chanted the spell.

The words wrapped themselves around her and Emily swallowed desperately. Why was her mother putting a spell on her? "Please don't take my magic away!" she cried. "It's only a little bit. I never meant to do anything wrong. Sasha needed help. And then I made a mouse, and that was all."

The spell flowered around her, and Emily

gasped as something moved, deep inside. It felt like it was lodged inside her heart, and her eyes filled with tears. It *was* the magic! Her mother was taking it away.

"No. . ." she sobbed. "It's mine. I loved it. . . Please let me keep it. It's only little!"

But the tiny spot inside her heart didn't grow cold as she had thought it would. It stayed warm and flickering, like a candle flame. Emily could feel it burn up more strongly as her mother's magic joined with it, glowing inside her. Emily blinked away her tears and looked at her mother, surprised.

Eva was smiling at her. Her eyes were open now, but she was crying too, fat tears spilling over on to her cheeks.

"How did you do it?" she murmured, letting go of one of Emily's hands and reaching up to stroke her face. "Your own magic – completely different to anything the others have. Small, yes, but real. And sweet, Emily! So sweet and strong. . ."

"I thought you were going to take it away!" Emily threw her arms around her mother's shoulders, hugging her gratefully.

"How could I?" Eva sounded almost cross. "It was a gift, Emily. From the house you've grown up in. It isn't for us to tear it out of you."

"But you must be careful how you use it," Ash added, leaning close to them. "Your mother's tested the magic and found it's true – there's nothing dangerous inside you. But that doesn't

make it safe. Any magic can be dangerous if used the wrong way."

Emily nodded, and glanced over her mother's shoulder at Robin and Sasha. Was this the time to tell her parents about Lory and Dan and their terrible plan? But what if telling the secret brought all the dreadful force of Lory's spell down on Lark?

Robin's face scrunched up worriedly, so that for a second he looked like a rabbit. Sasha seemed thinner and more insubstantial than ever, as though the thought of telling frightened her.

Then Robin shook his head reluctantly. It wasn't safe. They would have to stop Lory some other way. On their own.

7

"She's been ages," Lark muttered, glancing at the clock on the kitchen wall.

"What time did she go out?" Emily asked, jabbing uncertainly at the top of her toffee-sponge cake. It wasn't done. She put it back in the oven and came to sit down with Lark and Robin. Even cooking, which always cheered her up, wasn't working today.

Sasha, who had been standing by the sink

and letting water drip over her hands, pulled out a chair opposite Emily. Their parents hadn't actually said she was allowed to stay – but it was as if they were pretending not to see her.

"I don't know when Lory went!" Lark wailed. "I didn't see, and it's not as if she told me she was going, is it? I haven't spoken to her since yesterday. I've hardly even seen her."

After the fight, Lory had stayed in her room all evening. She'd told their mum she wasn't feeling well, that she had a headache and she just wanted to be left alone. Then sometime that morning she'd disappeared out again.

"After what Lory did to you yesterday, I don't know why you're worrying about her." Robin shrugged.

"It wasn't Lory." Emily flicked through her recipe book, so as not to look at Robin and Lark. She had a feeling they were going to laugh at her. But she was sure now. As if saying it out loud had made her certain. It wasn't Lory who Lark had fought. Lory would never bind her sister in a spell like that. Emily nodded to herself. She couldn't bring herself to believe that the real Lory would do such a thing.

"Looked like Lory to me!" Robin snorted.

"I know. But she's being made to do all this stuff. I'll bet you anything. Chocolate brownies every day for life."

Robin looked up at her sharply and Brownie's small, whiskery face appeared over the edge of the table, staring eagerly at Emily.

"You think Dan put a spell on Lory, then?" Lark asked curiously. There was a hopeful tone in her voice too, as though she wanted to believe it. She and Lory had always been so close. Emily couldn't imagine how it must feel to have her twin suddenly turn on her like this.

"Mm-hm. Think about it," Emily said. "She complained about him like anything, didn't she? Said he was a real pain, and she hated the way he kept turning up everywhere." Emily frowned. "And then he wrote that song. . ."

Emily's eyes widened. How many times had she heard it faintly floating out from Lory's room? How many times had Lory listened to it? He must have charmed her with the song! Lory was bound under a spell – a slow, gentle, but

clever and awfully strong spell that had started a long time ago, when Dan Hargreaves first tried to charm the pretty Feather sisters.

"It was the song! It's a spell!" she gasped.

Lark stared at Emily, her eyes so dark with surprise they looked almost black, and then slowly, she began to smile, a huge grin of relief. "You're right! She listened to it loads. I kept hearing her playing it on her laptop – even though she said it was terrible. It drove me mad. She kept putting it on, as if she didn't even notice she was doing it. That's when I started leaving her on her own in her room."

"Exactly." Emily nodded.

"The song was a spell?" Sasha asked.

"I think so. Specially designed to trap Lory."

Robin scowled at her. "That's so stupid it's almost definitely right, and now we won't get the chocolate brownies." Brownie stared up at Emily, his fat moustache of white whiskers drooping sadly.

"If we can get rid of Dan, I promise I'll make brownies once a week," Emily told him. She reached out a finger and dipped it in the spilled sugar on the table, holding it out for the tiny mouse to nibble. "I don't mind. I like making them." She drew a pattern in the sugar, which made Brownie glare at her disapprovingly. "If we don't stop Lory and Dan, everything could change! Dad could get in real trouble, couldn't he?"

Lory nodded. "If he didn't do his duty properly,

he could be called back. Someone else would be guardian instead. Dad could be put in prison, even."

"Yes. . . And then you'd all have to go home," Emily murmured, still playing with the sugar. "I don't know if you'd even be allowed to take me."

"Of course we'd take you!" Robin gasped.

"Would you? If Dad's already in disgrace? He and Mum won't exactly be in a good place for asking favours, will they? I've already got Lark and Lory into trouble. Lady Anstis is really powerful at court, isn't she? What if she tells the king not to let them bring me?" Emily shrugged. "I mean, that's not the only reason — I don't want Dan to hurt Lory, or use her to do something awful. But I can't help thinking about all this other

stuff as well." She tried to smile at Robin. "Total chocolate brownie shortage then. I bet they don't know how to make them in your world."

"I don't only love you because you make cake, you know!" Robin said crossly.

"Mm-hm, she makes really good biscuits as well." Lark put her arm round Emily's shoulders. "Stop playing with the sugar and look at us, stupid."

Reluctantly, Emily glanced up to find her brother and sister gazing down at her. They were half in their fairy form, their faces and their huge eyes glowing.

"How long have you known her?" Robin demanded, nodding at Sasha, who made a face back at him.

"Um, well. . . Not long, really. A couple of weeks?"

"Exactly. And you didn't leave her on the other side, in danger, did you? I know you're a lot nicer than I am, Emily, but I'm not totally heartless."

"And Mum and Dad aren't either," Lark added. "No one is leaving you behind. Anyway," she sighed. "I don't know what I'd do if I had to choose. I can't imagine living over there. But to stay here – I mean, in this world, but not in this house – without any magic at all, that would be too hard. We might all have to go rogue, somehow. Mum and Dad have been here so long I don't think they're true fairies any more. Not in the way they think, anyway."

"So stop panicking about being left behind

and go back to being the genius who spotted Dan's plot," Robin ordered. "Why didn't we see what that song was?"

"I was too busy stuffing my hair in my ears," Lark muttered. "What are we going to do? She really has been gone hours now. At least three hours, I think."

Robin suddenly jumped up. "Did she definitely leave the house?"

"I told you, I don't know. . ." Lark began angrily. "Oh! The attic!" She flung herself away from the table so fast her chair tipped over, and leaped into the air, her wings exploding from her shoulders in a fountain of soft grey-brown feathers. She beat them furiously, swirling in the air, so that Emily's curls lifted in the wind.

136

Then she shot out of the kitchen, spiralling up the stairs like some huge trapped bird.

"Go on!" Emily sighed. "You can fly, I don't mind. We'll see you up there."

Robin shrugged, tucking Brownie into the zip pocket of his camo shorts. "We're already at least three hours behind Lory. Lark's just being dramatic. I'll walk. Stupid flying indoors anyway – I always hit things."

Emily, Robin and Sasha hurried up the stairs, finding the small dark door to the attic swinging open. The shadowy steps made Emily's heart beat a little faster – she still loved the thought of a treasure trove full of magical secrets.

"Hmm. Where'd Lark go?" Robin asked, standing at the top of the attic stairs and looking around.

137

Emily and Sasha peered over his shoulder. It was late afternoon and thick, honeyed sunlight was pouring through the small windows, leaving golden pools on the dusty floor. The attic seemed to run all along the top of the house, Emily realized, just under the roof, so the ceilings were slanted and low. It was just as she had imagined – piled to the rafters with strange old stuff. At first look, it was like any other family's junk room – bags full of outgrown clothes, wooden boxes packed with unwanted books, an old bird cage, a little row of tiny shoes. But when Emily crouched down to inspect a pile of books, she saw that the one on the top had a green leather cover stamped with gold letters. She couldn't read the title – the letters wouldn't stand still long enough. It was as

though Emily had to open the book to make it decide what it was going to be. She wasn't quite brave enough.

"Where's Lark gone?" she asked, reluctantly turning away from the pile. "Through another door?"

"I don't know," Robin murmured back. "And I'm sure Lory's been here too, not long ago. I can feel her. I thought she and Dan would be up here looking for that secret door and Lark would be having a go at them. I was all set to be breaking up another fight. Where are they all?"

"I don't know. . ." Emily replied unhappily. A cloud must have passed across the sun – the golden light had darkened now, and the attic had turned shadowy and dim. Suddenly, she had the strongest sense that something was wrong.

"I don't like it," she added, swallowing. It felt like there was a solid lump of fright stuck in her throat.

"Me neither," Robin stepped back closer to her. "Emily, I think we have to go and tell Mum and Dad what's going on."

"But the spell!" Emily shuddered. Watching Lark twisting in pain from the burning spell had been so awful. She wasn't sure she could bear to make something like that happen again.

"I know. . ." Robin shook his head worriedly. "I don't want to hurt Lark, but everything up here feels dark and horrible. You can feel it too, can't you?"

Sasha nodded. "Yes. I can feel it too. Some sort of treacherous spell, cruel, and dark."

"Treachery?" Emily gasped. "Does that mean

Lory's done something else awful to Lark? Where are they?"

Here. . .

It was the faintest whisper, so faint that they felt it rather than heard it, from over in the far corner of the room.

Lark was lying behind a cluster of battered chairs, her fingers reaching towards an old wooden chest. Her wings were torn and battered, like a sea bird caught in a storm. The beautiful soft brown glow of them was gone, leaving the feathers grey and dusty.

"What happened?" Emily cried, crouching down beside her.

"I tried to follow them. He found the door. Look." She stretched her fingers out another

painful fraction and tried to point. "The chest. Dan left a spell to stop us. He must have known we'd try to follow them."

"Are you all right?" Emily asked, hesitantly stroking Lark's dusty feathers and wishing she knew a healing magic.

"I will be. I just can't move. It's a binding spell fixed to the door . . . to cripple whoever tries to follow after them. He must have thought we'd be together, but I got all of it."

"Can't we undo it?" Robin asked, brushing his fingers over the dusty boards around her, trying to find the limits of the spell.

Lark wriggled helplessly and sighed. "I don't think so. It's strong. Like . . . like I'm set in stone, or something."

"I don't think it'll come undone until they come back through the door," Sasha whispered apologetically, dropping one sparkling water droplet from her finger into the corner of Lark's mouth.

Emily watched her sister's cheeks flush a little pinker and her eyes grow brighter from Sasha's magic, and frowned. "We'd better go and get them back, then."

Emily crept a little closer, looking sideways at the chest. It seemed slippery and dangerous, as if she would fall right through the magical doorway if she dared to look at it straight on.

The chest was made of a dark wood, bound with heavy iron bands – as though the contents had to be sealed tightly inside. The lid was thrown

back against the hinges, and squinting sideways into the open chest, Emily could see the world beyond – great masses of trees, and the river flowing along between them, glimmering. "It leads into the forest again," she said. The doors she had opened before had been the same, opening on to dark pathways between the trees.

"All the doors do," Robin murmured, leaning cautiously over to look. "The forest is the heart of our world. All the strength and life comes from the trees and the river. Dan will still be in among the trees somewhere, I bet. He'll need to gather his magic before he attacks the king."

Emily swallowed fearfully. "Do you think we

might be able to stop him, then? I mean, I was just hoping we could get Lory away from him, but do you think we could stop the plot as well?"

Robin looked at her and shrugged helplessly. "What, you and me?"

Emily sighed. "I suppose not."

"Me too," Sasha whispered faintly.

"You can't!" Emily reminded her, shaking her head. "The hunt, remember? If they catch your scent, they'll go back to chasing you again. It isn't safe for you to go through."

"And it's safe for you?" Sasha hissed crossly. "If you go, I go, Emily! You don't know the forest and I do! I've rescued you once, and you've rescued me. We're evens. I'm not going

to let you get snapped up by some nasty little wisp who wants that scrap of magic inside you for her own!"

"What about the hunt then?" Robin demanded.

Sasha shrugged. "We'd better just find your sister fast, I suppose . . . and keep an eye on the door back. Let's hope he hasn't taken her far."

"You can track her," Lark whispered faintly. "Look. She left a message. Caught in the hinges."

"What?" Robin and Emily peered closely at the wooden chest, Emily squeezing her eyes into slits to see better. The chest seemed to waver between their world, where it was a battered wooden box, and the fairy land, where it opened out into the forest, a great dark rent torn through a hollow tree.

Caught in a crack in the bark was a golden feather, silken and glinting. A feather from a fairy's wings.

Emily ran her finger down the rippled edge of the feather and her mind filled with panicked images. They were jumbled and hurried but eager, as though Lory had been desperate to pass her message on.

Emily could see Lory had passed through the door, feeling the strong magic of her homeland, and that she had come to her senses. Suddenly, she realized what she had done.

The feather twisted and quivered under Emily's frightened fingers, and her eyes filled with tears as she saw its message.

Lory had summoned all her magic, but too

late. Dan had been too strong and she couldn't escape. The feather had been torn out in a last desperate gasp as she fought the enemy dragging her through the door.

8

"If you take it," Lark whispered weakly, "you should be able to track her."

"How?" Emily asked, looking curiously at the feather.

"The same way the hunt works," Robin explained. "And how I could feel Lory had been here. Everyone's magic is different, and you can track the essence of them, if you're careful.

Having the feather will help, it's a part of Lory's magic. It should lead us to her."

Emily nodded. She was still stroking the feather, and she did feel as though she was holding a part of Lory. It seemed to wriggle in her fingers, eager and determined and rebellious. It tugged at her grip, as though it wanted to vanish through the door after the rest of itself. Robin was right – she knew the feather would lead them to Lory.

Emily swallowed. "We'd better go and get them back," she said again. "Does this spell really need Dan back here to undo it?" she asked Sasha, hoping she'd say no.

"I think so." Sasha sighed and ran a gentle hand over Lark, shivering as she met the stony magic of the spell. "Spells are like that, sometimes. You

have to balance one thing against another. And almost always it's the person who puts the spell on who has to take it off again. I don't know how he made this one. It's old, I think. We might be able to find some way to break it, but it would be better just to make him come back through the door. Then it'll just undo."

Emily nodded. It did make sense that Dan would have to break his own spell, unfortunately. "Come on then," she murmured, stepping a little closer to the chest. Even as frightened as she was, and worried about her sisters, her stomach still gave a little jump of excitement, as though she was in a fast lift. She could hear the trees rustling in the warm wind, now she was closer, and the river, shallow at the edges, was rippling over

stones, chattering to itself. She smiled. It was the sort of thing people just said about water, in the human world, but over there, who knew? Perhaps the water really was talking.

Sasha was smiling too, one hand reaching out towards the chest with a painful eagerness. For the first time, Emily wondered how much it hurt for her to be away from her home, from the strong, rushing water of her river. It wasn't just her home, it was part of her. A garden pond, even in a half-magical garden, couldn't ever be the same.

Emily hated to remind Sasha that the river could never be her home again, but she had to. "We must be careful," she said gently. "How long will it take for the hunt to catch your scent again?

152

I mean, they could be anywhere. The other side of the world? Maybe they won't even notice?"

"They will," Sasha and Robin said grimly together, and even Lark gave a sad little nod.

"I won't have long," Sasha murmured. "The hunt will sense that I'm back and they don't run the way you do, Emily. They'll fly, if they must. They have horses and they'll gallop through the air."

Emily sighed. "You shouldn't come with us. But you're going to anyway, aren't you, whatever I say? Let's hope you're right and Dan hasn't gone far."

"This spell must have taken a lot of his strength," Lark croaked, raising herself a little on one elbow. "He's lived without his real magic for years and years, if he's been in exile here. He'll be weak now. He can't have gone far."

153

"He's probably just beyond the door." Sasha nodded.

"Waiting for us!" Emily said it before she thought, and then wished she hadn't. It wasn't helpful.

Robin glared at her, but Sasha shook her head. "No. The binding spell, remember? He'll think we're all caught. We should be able to take him by surprise."

"Um. . ." Emily looked uncertainly between Robin and Sasha. "How exactly are we going to do that? I know we think he's weakened, but he's still one of the great lords, isn't he? He was part of the fairy court if he really is Lady Anstis's brother."

"So am I," Robin pointed out.

Emily blinked at him. "No, you're not."

"I would be if I lived there. By right of birth.

154

Lark and Lory would be too." He smirked at Emily. "You don't know what I could do if I didn't have Mum and Dad hovering around, making sure I don't start any magic and break all our rules."

Emily eyed him uncertainly. "Really?" He was still her littler brother, even if she had seen him with wings. . .

"Mmm-hmm. And I'm used to living in the human world. I always have. Not like him." Robin flexed his fingers and grinned wolfishly.

Emily nibbled her bottom lip. Robin being boastful was nothing new, but was he really as strong as he thought? "Let's just go," she muttered. "But promise me you won't do anything stupid."

Robin shrugged and smiled. "I can't help it, Emily. I can't do any magic over here. Once we go

through that door I can do anything I like. . . It's exciting!"

"Lory. . ." Lark wheezed, trying to reach for his foot. "Remember you're there for Lory!"

"I know." Robin crouched down next to her. "We'll get her back, don't worry." Then he sprang back up, grabbing Emily's hand, and Sasha's. "Let's go. We don't want to give Dan any more time than we have to. And remember, we stick together as we go through."

Emily nodded. She had no intention of going off on her own, however wonderful it was to be going back to that entrancing world. Now that they were really about to step through the door, she wasn't sure if her stomach was jumping because she was excited, or terrified. Sasha's face

looked pale and pinched but Robin truly seemed not to be scared at all. He was dancing on tiptoe as he walked around the chest, and then slowly he delicately stepped inside.

Emily felt a sharp tug on her arm and stepped hurriedly after him, scared to be left behind. There was a strange moment of blackness and cold, and then she was there, up to her knees in bright, curled ferns, the gaping hole of the hollow tree at her back. She couldn't see home through it, but then she supposed that wasn't really surprising. It was a secret door, after all.

Robin's wings had grown, she realized. She hadn't seen them spring out of his shoulders. She glanced at Sasha and caught her breath. The water fairy glittered in the sunlight, her hair

rippling down her back in a green-gold stream. Her bare toes were scrunched in the damp ferns, as though even that faint touch of water was breathing new life into her.

Emily shook herself. "Where is he?" she whispered to Robin and Sasha. The wood seemed to stretch on for ever, full of hiding places. And then she felt the feather twitch in her hand. "Look!" She held it out, watching it quiver and curl on her palm. If she squinted sideways a little, she could almost see a thin, golden trail, like a thread, leading away through the trees.

Treading as softly as they could, they crept between the huge trees. Emily found it hard to concentrate on the thin, thread-like trail – there was so much else to see. And to be seen by. A

tiny butterfly creature swooped down from the branches above them, its wings fluttering and blurring in the sunlight. It – she? – hovered in front of Emily, staring at her curiously, until Robin flapped her away with one sweep of his huge wings.

"What was that?" Emily breathed, watching the tiny thing twirl away, chittering angrily. It hadn't been just a butterfly – it had had a face, and bright, greedy little eyes.

"Something that could be off telling Dan we're here. Hurry up. Where's the thread?" Robin frowned down at the feather, trying to see the trail against the bars of shadow and light falling down through the trees.

"Look. . ." Sasha pointed between two trees,

out into a clearing, carpeted with white, star-like flowers.

"Nice. . ." Emily agreed, but then she saw what Sasha was really pointing at, and gasped.

Hanging from a smaller tree in the centre of the clearing, pretty as a picture in a cloud of pink and white blossom, was a small, golden cage. It swung gently in the soft breeze and petals floated down around it, like scented snow.

It was probably the prettiest prison anyone had ever seen, and inside it was slumped a tiny orange and gold and crimson bird.

"Lory!" Emily gasped, recognizing the patterns on the bird's half-spread wings. She started to run out across the star-like flowers, but Robin grabbed her wrist, hauling her back.

"Watch it! We don't know where he is!"

"Oh. . ." Emily stopped, looking around anxiously. Robin was right. Dan could be hiding anywhere. "I didn't think. . . How are we going to get to her then?"

"We should go around the edge of the clearing," Sasha whispered. "Behind the trees."

"We'll probably walk right into him," Robin muttered. But he started to creep round the next large oak tree as he said it, his wings tucked tightly against his back, as though he were trying to make himself as small as possible. For a moment Emily wondered if that was what they should do – make themselves tiny. She was sure Robin and Sasha could do it. But perhaps it would use up magic that they needed to save for rescuing Lory. And if

they were beetle-sized, it would be horribly easy for someone to tread on them.

"We're coming, Lory," Emily whispered, reaching out one hand to the tiny bird. She hated to turn away from her. The bird's wings were drooping so sadly, so hopelessly. So unlike her stroppy, confident sister. She looked as though she had given up – but surely she was expecting them to rescue her? Did she think they wouldn't follow her after the way she had behaved? Or perhaps she thought they would all have been caught in the trap spell on the chest. Then there would be no one to come after her until it was too late.

Emily shuddered. They could have been caught so easily. It was pure luck that Lark had dashed up to the attic ahead of them and sprung the spell.

She glanced fearfully over her shoulder, wondering if Dan had set any other traps.

"Can you see anything?" Sasha breathed, looking at her worriedly, and Emily shook her head. "You?"

Sasha sighed. "I keep thinking I do, but it's just the wind shaking the trees. Or I can hear the river."

"All I can hear is you," Robin hissed crossly, flapping one hand at them. "Shut up!"

"I wish we knew where Dan was," Emily whispered, ignoring Robin. "I hate thinking that he might be creeping up on us. Can't we tell where he might be? Like with Lory and the feather?"

"No!" Robin glared at her. "We don't have any of his magic to follow, do we? Look, let's just get

163

to Lory. If we can get her out of that cage it'll probably bring him running. Then we can try and fight him, and let's just hope he's still weak from his exile." He peered through the branches towards the blossom tree and the sparkling cage. "It all seems a lot more real now we're here," he admitted reluctantly. "If he's managed to get his strength back, we might just have to grab Lory and run. . ."

"And leave him to try and overthrow the king?" Emily hissed. "You want him and his evil sister in charge over here? Anyway, we need to take Dan back with us to break the spell on Lark." Then her eyes widened and she clutched Robin's wrist.

"What?"

"We *do* have some of his magic!"

Robin and Sasha stared at her, and she nodded excitedly. "We do! The song, remember! The song he wrote for Lory. That was a spell. Can't we use it against him somehow?"

Robin frowned, his huge eyes narrowing. "Can you remember it?"

Emily laughed out loud, and then slapped her hand over her mouth. "Sorry. Yes, of course I can! I heard it often enough, didn't I? She played it over and over. I could probably sing you the whole thing!"

Robin nodded. "All right. Go on then. But quietly! And come to the edge of the trees. I reckon he's hiding somewhere close to Lory – we need to be able to see if he reacts."

Emily nodded and looked out across the clearing,

fixing her eyes on the tiny crimson bird. Robin and Sasha stood beside her, close enough to touch. She took a breath and started to sing, waveringly at first. She liked to sing, but usually only to herself, or singing along to music with Rachel. It was odd to sing on her own – and especially this song with the sugary lyrics she hated. But after a couple of lines, Emily forgot to be shy. She could almost see the words coming out of her mouth, twining round each other and spiralling out into the sunlit clearing. Her eyes widened and she kept singing, glancing round at Robin.

He nodded eagerly at her – he could see it too. It was like the golden thread of Lory's magic that they'd followed. The song became a soft, greenish mist, trailing through the bars of green-gold light,

looping its way over to the pink and white blossom of the tree.

It wreathed itself around the glittering cage, and the scarlet bird lifted its head, sitting up on its perch, its tail feathers twitching.

Emily caught her breath. Lory knew that they were here. From across the clearing, she saw the little bird's dark eyes glint and her beak open. Lory began to sing, adding a chirruping trill to the song, changing it a little, making it stronger.

"She's adding to the spell!" Robin whispered. "Dan never thought of that when he made her a bird. Singing's about the only thing she can do to fight back."

"Look!" Sasha pointed. "In the tree, just above her."

The greenish mist was shot through with golden lights now, and it was gathering closely around the branch above Lory, where a glittering chain secured the cage. And over it lay a white figure, stretched out along the branch, one paw wrapped around the chain.

"A cat!" Robin hissed, as Emily sang the last few words of the song. "Why's Dan disguised himself as a cat?"

"Because they're the best way to catch a bird? And because that white fur is hidden in the blossoms, I suppose. We didn't see him before, did we? Emily shrugged, still catching her breath from the song. "I think he's asleep," she added, leaning out from behind the huge tree. "His eyes are closed, anyway."

"No wonder Gruff couldn't stand him," Robin

muttered, as he trod softly out into the clearing, the starry flowers hardly crushed at all under his feet. The two girls followed, creeping closer and closer to the tree – close enough that the sweet scent of the blossom seemed to wrap itself all round them. It was too sweet.

At last they were right under the tree, the heavy branches drooping down. Lory was in her cage, hopping agitatedly on the perch, just above their heads.

"He *is* asleep," Emily said, in the merest breath of a whisper, trying not to gag as the sickly scent of the flowers stuck in her throat.

Robin and Sasha nodded, and Emily stood on tiptoe, reaching up to the door of the cage. The mist of green magic was still wrapped round the

white cat, who was stretched dozing on the branch, but his paw was over the chain – if the cage shook, he was sure to wake.

Sasha gently placed both hands around the bottom of the cage, holding it steady while Emily reached for the catch. It was a fiddly little thing, a loop of wire that had to be unhooked. All the while Lory was perched just on the other side of the pretty gilded door, her feathers trembling and her eyes fixed desperately on Emily.

Emily had just managed to pull the little door open, it creaking on its delicate hinges, when she heard Sasha gasp and saw Robin leap into the air beside her.

A fat white paw, edged with dagger-sharp claws, shot down, clanging the gilded door shut.

Emily screamed as the claws raked down her hand and gouged Sasha's arm, but she kept hold of the door, pulling it open again as she scrambled backwards, trying to avoid the slashing paws.

The fragile cage buckled and the door sheared away from its hinges. The white cat sprang down from the branch, hissing furiously, and slipping on the smooth wire sides of the cage. He was trying to block the door, but Sasha and Emily shoved him away, and Robin had him round the shoulders, yanking him up into the air, with his tail lashing furiously.

"Get back to the door!" Robin yelled, as the cat twisted and yowled and slashed at his face, and Lory twirled up into the white blossoms, chirruping in delight.

171

"No!" It was a strange mixture of hissing and mewing and words, as the cat twisted and began to turn into something else – a figure with a cat-like face. It struggled against Robin's grip, growing larger and heavier every second, until at last he had to let it slide out of his fingers.

"Sasha, no! Get away from him!" Emily yelled as she saw the water fairy dart in close to the squirming mass of white fur, which was rapidly becoming a tall figure in a white velvet cloak. "What are you doing?"

"You'll see!" Sasha gasped. She had her gashed arm held up against her chest, the silvery fabric of her dress swathed around it. But as she leaned over Dan, she unwrapped the seeping cuts and stroked them down his face, and over the velvet,

whimpering as the cuts dripped silver. Then she staggered back, glancing fearfully through the trees.

"What is it?" Emily caught Sasha as she reeled, and Lory landed on her shoulder, singing a strange anxious little call, over and over, and brushing the deep scratches with her gold and scarlet tail feathers.

"The hunt. . ." Sasha murmured, jerking her head towards the trees. "My scent. They know I'm here."

Lory took off again, flying a circle round their heads and screeching. Robin grabbed Sasha's uninjured arm, dragging her towards the trees, half-running, half-flying, with great worried flaps of his wings.

173

"Better run, then!"

"Yes." Sasha began to stumble through the flowers, but she kept looking back to Dan, now almost in his full fairy form and glaring after them as he knelt beneath the tree. His wings were growing now too, great white wings, like some sort of eagle. He looked like a warrior angel – except for the snarling grimace of anger on his face.

"Hurry! They'll catch you!" Emily panted, trying to haul Sasha on. She could hear the hunters, screeching triumphantly as they galloped on horseback, through the air this time, the hounds baying as they caught the scent. "Where's the door? Where's the hollow tree?"

"There!" Robin pointed ahead, and then risked a

glance behind them. "But they're close," he groaned. "They're gaining, I can see them above the clearing."

Emily pounded through the ferns and reached out desperately for the gnarled bark of the ancient tree, gasping and coughing for breath. "Go through!" she screamed to Lory as she tried to drag Sasha through the gaping hole – the door. The scarlet bird shot through the door with a shrill cry of delight, but Sasha dug her nails into the bark and turned.

"What is it?" Emily asked angrily, pulling at her. "We can't wait, they'll catch you." She swallowed down the ball of fear rising in her throat. "I know we're supposed to bring Dan back with us, but we'll do something else to free Lark. I don't know what, but we will. Won't we?" she begged Robin.

"He's coming. . ." Robin wasn't listening to her. He was hovering above the door, his wings beating in a grey-brown blur. "He's following us! What's he doing that for? He's been trying to get back into this world for hundreds of years!"

Stumbling wearily through the tall ferns was a white figure, a tall lord in a swirling velvet cloak – a beautiful garment that wasn't really made for running in. It flapped around his ankles as he bounded, still cat-like, towards the door.

"Is he after Lory?" Emily whispered, hunching back against the tree. Dan's eyes were still a cat's, green, and slit-pupilled, and he looked furious.

"They're after *him*. . ." Sasha giggled, and then

she swept around and pulled Emily through the door so that the pair of them tumbled out into the attic, next to Lark and Lory.

"You're not a bird any more!" Emily cried, hugging Lory tightly.

"The door took the spell off. What's happened to Lark?" Lory demanded, squeezing Emily for a moment and then breaking away anxiously. "Look at her – she's asleep and I can't wake her." Lory's eyes filled with tears. "Is that what I did to her, burning the feather? I didn't want to, Emily. He made me, somehow."

Emily nodded. "It was the song. He bewitched you with it. But then he left a sort of spell fixed to the door, to trap us if we followed you. That's what got Lark."

Robin fluttered out of the chest. "He's still following me. Sasha, what did you do?"

Sasha looked up from binding strips of silvery cloth around the deep scratches on her arm and smiled. "I gave him my scent. He was transforming back into his real self when I touched him. That's why he's coming back – because he doesn't have a choice."

Robin stared at her. "The hunt are after him?"

"The hunt are after him." Sasha nodded. "The hounds are confused – they know he isn't me, but the scent is there, you see. He can't get rid of it. So he'll have to escape through the door. And that will break the spell on Lark. I hope," she added, looking worriedly at the sisters. Lory was curled

over Lark now, patting at her greyish cheek and whispering to her.

"Will they follow him?" Emily asked anxiously. She could hear the hunters, shouting and hooting with excitement just beyond the door. There were footsteps too, getting closer and closer. "It's a secret door, you said! It isn't guarded, so they could come through too, couldn't they?"

Robin stared at her. "No. . ." he said. He looked at the chest, frowning, and then added, "We need to shut it. Let him get through to break the spell, and then slam it so the hunt can't follow." He moved back closer to the chest, putting his hands on the lid. "Hold the other side," he told Emily. "And get ready to slam it shut. He's coming!"

The tall white figure shot out into the room gasping and collapsed on the floor. "Not here. . ." he moaned feebly. "Not again."

The sharp bang of the chest slamming down echoed around the dusty room, and Emily sat down on it, trying to think heavy thoughts.

"Bolt it!" she yelped to Robin, and he slid the heavy well-oiled hasps down and shoved an old walking stick through the holes.

"No one's getting in through that," he said triumphantly. Then he giggled. "Someone's swearing blue murder on the other side of there, I can just hear. But it's fading. The door's closed on both sides now."

The colour and life were rushing back into Lark's face and then she sprang up, with Lory

beside her. They leaned over Dan, their faces looking identical for once, sharp and furious.

The white figure on the floor squirmed back a little and stared up at them uncertainly.

"Why did I ever think you were good-looking?" Lory snarled.

"He made quite a handsome cat," Emily said, leaning over to see.

Dan hissed and muttered. Being a cat seemed to suit him. His nails were still long and sharp, and he had hardly any chin.

"He should stay as one. Gruff could keep him in order," Lark said angrily. Then she looked round at Lory. "We could do that," she said thoughtfully. "If we're quick. Before he gathers his strength again."

"But Mum and Dad. . ." Lory began. "They'll feel the spell." Then she sighed. "I suppose I'll have to tell them anyway."

"They ought to be pleased," Robin put in. "He was going to overthrow the king and we stopped him. They can't really complain! In fact, it sounds to me like we ought to get a raise in our pocket money."

"Hold hands." Lory reached out to Emily and Sasha, wrapping her hand very gently around Sasha's damaged arm.

They gathered in a ring around Dan, who was still squirming unpleasantly on the dusty boards, tangled in his silly velvet cloak. Emily wondered for a moment how she could have been frightened of him, and then she caught his eye and shivered.

He was growing stronger again as they watched, starting to sit up, his face becoming harder and prouder.

"What do we do?" she whispered to Lory.

"Imagine him as a cat again. I'll do the rest." Her eyes were glowing, Emily noticed – yellowish-gold, like an owl's.

Emily thought hard, remembering him stretched out in the tree, the soft white paws hiding sharp dagger-claws inside. Then she shut her eyes. She didn't want that sort of cat. She did her best to think about purring, and lap-cats, and a little collar with a fish-shaped tag, engraved *Dantis*.

An angry hiss startled her into opening her eyes again. A small white cat was sharpening his

claws against the wooden boards, his green eyes sparkling with anger and his fur a little damp-looking.

Lark reached down and picked him up, holding him out at arm's length and smirking as he hissed and spat. "We'd better go and meet your new owners, kitty," she said, turning as she heard hurrying footsteps on the stairs. "It's all right. Dad's always wanted a cat."

"You'll have to be careful with Brownie," Emily reminded Robin, looking at his pockets and wondering which one had a mouse in.

"Mmm." Robin nodded. "If I find that white thug anywhere near my room, I'll post him back through one of the doors. Whatever that means with the hunt."

"So – he can never go back?" Emily looked round at Sasha, who shrugged.

"I don't know for sure. But his scent will always carry a little bit of mine, I think." She wandered over to the tiny window. "So the hunt would still chase him. Probably neither of us can ever go back."

"Do you mind very much?" Emily asked her in a small voice. She leaned on the windowsill next to Sasha, peering out into the garden at the trees and the tiny pond far below.

Sasha wrapped her good arm around Emily's shoulders. "A little – some days more than others. It's a lot more exciting here, anyway. Fish don't have these sort of adventures."

Emily giggled. "I suppose not. And there's better cake here, too."

"True. And there are chances to go back, like today."

Emily nodded. "It's worth it, isn't it?" she whispered. "Even though it's not safe."

"Never safe," Sasha agreed. She smiled and turned as Ash and Eva came hurrying through the attic door, staring in horror at the furry white fairy lord in Lark's arms. "Maybe we have the best of both worlds, Emily, don't you think?"